kamea

By Jeri Howe

Kamea

Copyright ©2012 by Jeri Howe

Requests for information should be directed to jeri@jerihowe.com. More information available at: kameathebook.com

This book is a work of fiction. Any resemblance to actual persons, living or dead, is entirely coincidental.

Cover Design by Taylor Vanden Hoek – taylorvdh.com
Photo of author by Jennifer Howe

Thank you...

To my husband, Jason: for believing in me and bringing this to print.

To my Mom, Carol Van Kampen: for reading everything I write before anyone else does (red pen in hand!) ... This is our work!

To my Dad, Hank Van Kampen: for supporting me and for asking me again and again, "What is happening with Kamea?"

To my daughter, Hannah: for editing, discussion question advice, and ideas for sequels.

To my son, Lucas: for helping me with the "fight scene."

To my sister, Jodi Van Kampen: for supporting and encouraging me.

To Ann Merlino: for hosting a pilot study with *Kamea* and the companion *Journey Guide* at Lakeshore Vineyard Church (and thanks to all the pilot participants!)

To Pastor Paul Bradford, D.Min.: for his insightful Theological Review of Kamea and his creative suggestions.

To my prayer team: thank you for partnering with me through prayer!

And to Jesus, my precious Jesus, who saw I was lost in the darkness and rescued me and brought me into the Kingdom of Light.

Dedicated to Hannah and Lucas...

Preface

KAMEA is a medieval fantasy, a story of one woman's journey from the Dominion of Darkness into the Kingdom of Light. It is meant to be enjoyed with a cup of your favorite warm drink in a cozy spot where you can let it paint pictures on the canvas of your mind.

Like all fiction, it is devised to stimulate the imagination of the reader. It also may uncover doubts and inspire hope. While reading KAMEA, some people may recognize the story as being inspired by the Bible. The conversations and metaphors in this novel are not meant to replace or even explain the Bible, but rather to inspire one to find out what the Bible really says. To this end, superscripts will be found throughout the text and can be looked up in the endnotes. There are more than two hundred endnotes in this novel that reference Bible verses.

My greatest dream in writing **Kamea** is that, as you read of Kamea's journey, you may take your own journey of self-discovery. To this end, I have made available a companion study, called the KAMEA JOURNEY GUIDE. More information is available at kameathebook.com or jerihowe.com.

Register your copy of Kamea here to get updates and irregular messages from the author:
http://www.kameathebook.com/register.html

A Note on Names

Many of the characters' names in KAMEA have special meaning. Pronunciations and definitions can be found in the back of the book among the endnotes.

To those in dark places...

...from one who has been there.

"FOR HE HAS
RESCUED US FROM THE
DOMINION OF DARKNESS
AND BROUGHT US INTO
THE KINGDOM
OF THE SON HE LOVES..."

COLOSSIANS 1:13 (NIV)

Prologue

THE LEGEND OF THE ONE AND ONLY

Before the ancient times began…long, long ago, beyond the reach of memory, in a time we can only touch with our imagination….in this era the Creator King was. He was there before… Before any of what we now call the world…Before anyone walked the paths of this life. What we know of this time comes shrouded in mystery… brought to us by elusive figures we call "the Keepers of the Legend."

No one knows exactly where the Keepers of the Legend come from or where they go… but at one time or another we have all heard one of them share their amazing story. They tell us that there came a time when the Creator King did his work. When he began the beginning. When he made all that has been made.[1]

The Keepers of the Legend tell us the world was beautiful then, full of light and hope and promise. The land overflowed with good things; it burst forth with abundant food and safety and companionship. There were joyful songs in the hearts of the people. Laughter was heard resounding in the hills.

But, alas, it would not always be so. Something occurred that changed everything. Something evil and sinister. Shortly after time began, something happened that changed the world from a place of great light to a place of shadows and confusion.

Among those fashioned by the Creator King was a dragon – the most beautiful and powerful being he had made. The dragon rebelled against the Creator King and turned from the only true light to the darkness. And when he did he spoke contagious ideas to trouble our minds. He inflamed our hearts with greed and our thoughts with fear. He raised suspicions about the Creator King, accusing him of wrongdoing and evil intentions. And we believed the dragon.[2] We agreed with him that the Creator King was unkind and lacking in generosity. As we trusted the dragon's twisted words, his influence over us grew and grew.

The once shadowy dragon now rose up, larger and more powerful in our eyes – a Great and Terrible Dragon. As he spoke his poisonous words to our hearts, arousing selfish, greedy and fearful thoughts within us, he deceived the entire world into rebelling against the good and noble Creator King. We threw off the King's authority, turned our back on him and went our own way.[3]

But after we, the people of this world, had revolted against the Creator King, the dragon betrayed us. Everyone, big and small, men and women, now served the Great and Terrible Dragon. We were deceived into fighting in his ongoing war against the Creator King.

For many years the dragon prowled the lands, always looking for someone to kill, something to destroy.[4] He relished the opportunity to squelch hope and worked hard to keep everyone in darkness. He seemed to grow and thrive in the shadows and in the fear and despair of the people. He was known to have the ability to take a shred of truth and weave it so craftily with threads of deception that his hearers were seemingly taken under a spell by his lies.[5] They were beguiled by him and took his thoughts for their own.

Some think that all live under the influence of his toxic falsehoods, that it affects how we all perceive the world, each other and ... even ourselves. And so, the world became a dark and hopeless place.[6] [7]

But that was not the end of the story.

The Keepers of the Legend always seem eager to share what happened next. Even so, as one of the Keepers whispers the Legend over a small fire under a thatched roof, you will see her eyes dart about, looking for dragon's breath to waft in through the windows. You see, he forbids the telling of the Legend... the Legend is not really about the Dragon at all...It belongs to another, to the One and Only.

The Legend speaks of an event years after the rebellion: a birth, an unusual birth of a boy child. His mother was one of us, one of this world. His father was a mystery. Some people thought the boy was conceived by magic, others by a miracle, still others gossiped that his father was the Almighty Creator King of the Glorious Kingdom of Light himself.[8]

Wonder surrounded the boy[9] because, although he was like us, he was unlike us. He looked and sounded and smelled like all of us, but there was one unmistakable difference: The boy child grew up and never did any wrong.[10] Never. Not once. Throughout his whole life in this shadowy, wicked world, he had done no harm, spoken no lies and participated in no evil schemes. Some loved him for it, some hated him for it. But there was no doubt, in this depraved world he was the one and only of his kind. And so he was called the One and Only.[11]

He was good to all, and many people were drawn to him. Hope and love seemed to shine from him, and his words were powerful and noble. Many just wanted to be near him, but he was not satisfied to just sit around. Something in him seemed to be moving him toward a larger goal. He knew why he had been born. He was driven to accomplish a purpose; a purpose larger than anyone had ever dared imagine. As time wore on, his intentions became clear. Namely, to defeat the Great and Terrible Dragon that ruled our world.

And so the day came when the One and Only determined that history was ripe and it was time to act. He went alone to confront the Great and Terrible Dragon, knowing he would find him prowling the lands and feeding his hunger for destruction. As he approached, the dragon sensed his arrival, and fiery breath began to pour forth from his nostrils. He had been waiting for an opportunity to destroy the One and Only for a very, very long time. The dragon hated him for his goodness. He hated that the One and Only had inspired hope in some of his slaves.

As they met on the cliffs of the dark mountains the battle began, each opponent fighting with all his strength. The dragon had terrible claws and teeth like spears. His scales were slick and shone in many colors, so he was hard to describe – his appearance was always changing. His eyes were intent on the One and Only, and he moved forward aggressively, attacking again and again. As the battle waged on, the One and Only seemed to have miraculous power to overcome the Great and Terrible Dragon, even though he had terrible claws and teeth and exhaled hateful fiery breath. The sword of the One and Only did not break or bend; it had the power to defeat the wicked one.

But then, the Legend says, the One and Only did something quite unexpected. In the midst of the battle he dropped his sword just as the Great and Terrible Dragon swiped at him with his jagged claws. The One and Only was thrown against the rocks, deep gashes freshly opened on his body. He was still alive, but he did not get up. The dragon goaded him, wanting him to get up and fight, but he did not. He lay there, bleeding, his breathing labored and difficult, awaiting the next blow. He did not say a word as the Great and Terrible Dragon taunted and mocked him. He was silent. The dragon kept beating him against rocks and trees. He threw him to the ground again and again. The beating covered much territory, and many witnessed it. None intervened. No one tried to help. And then, after intense pain and suffering,[12] the dragon tied the One and Only to a tree on the top of the mountain.

The sky grew dark. The One and Only remained, facing the oncoming storm, the purest and best being imaginable, now beaten beyond recognition. Then, as the lightning flashed, people said they thought they saw something else tied to the tree...a serpent...a serpent as wicked as the dragon himself. But as the lightning subsided it was clear that it was the One and Only who was tied to the tree. The storm raged. It was a storm unlike any before or since...it seemed as if all the wrath of the Creator King was being poured out against all the wickedness of the rebellious people onto this one good being[13]...the One and Only. As he remained tied to the tree, he cried out in anguish[14] – a cry that came from a profound pain, deep within his soul – his body shaking.

And then, the One and Only died. He cried out with his last breath, then his body went limp. [15] The earth shook, and boulders fell down the mountains.[16] For a moment, the world was in chaos, but then the storm stopped. All was still and dark. Silence filled the land.

The Keepers of the Legend will always stop here for a moment and look about the fire to catch the look of sadness in the eyes of the young ones who have never heard the legend before. A smile will begin to spread at the edges of their lips as they continue to share the Legend...

But that is not the end of the story. It is said that after the dragon left, those who loved the One and Only found his body, tenderly prepared it for burial and then placed it in a cave. But the body did not remain there.[17] You see, death could not hold him. The power in the One and Only was even more mighty than that of death. [18] He came back to life and appeared to several of his followers many times over several days.[19]

The young ones will look about the fire to see if others believe this could be true. Is the One and Only real? If he is not dead in the cave, then where is he? Inevitably, one will ask the question on everyone's hearts... "If he is alive, where is he now?"

Some think he lives among the stars in the sky, others think he did finally die. The Keepers of the Legend contend he has gone to the other Kingdom, the Kingdom of Light. They say he rules there with the Almighty One and wages battle daily against the Dominion of Darkness. Some gather in shadowy corners away from prying eyes and whisper stories that he rescues people from the Dominion of Darkness and brings them into the Kingdom of Light.[20] Most deny it as foolishness.

Yet, each of us secretly wonders in our hearts if the Legend is true.

CHAPTER 1

Everyone in the Dominion knew the Legend of the One and Only from the time they were very young. Fear of the Great and Terrible Dragon did not prevent the Keepers of the Legend from telling the ancient story around small fires while little children listened with wonder and fear.

Moncha could not remember the first time she had heard the story, nor could she understand why it haunted her dreams lately.

She was waking now, and the dream was fresh in her mind. "The Kingdom of Light."[21] At the thought of that Kingdom, a pleasant shudder went through Moncha's body, as it had ever since she was very young. She imagined the Kingdom as a place of indescribable beauty; a place that glowed with love and hope. Her dream began to grow dim, as dreams often do, and she found herself drifting back to the shadows and the despair of her life.

When Moncha was a child, she had wanted to believe there was a man so good, so powerful he could defeat the Great and Terrible Dragon. Everyone in the land was slave to the dragon and did his bidding. He had been waging a war against the forces of the opposing Kingdom for as long as history had been recorded, and he was always conscripting men to serve in his army. The dragon did not want to lose even one inch of his dominion, or one slave to the Kingdom of Light.

No one could remember a time when the Dominion of Darkness had not been fighting the Kingdom of Light. Everyone hated the war, and it had formed bitterness in their hearts against the opposing Kingdom. No one was sure why they fought. Perhaps, if the Legend was true, the Great and Terrible Dragon was afraid the One and Only would return to finish what he started and destroy him.[22] But it was only a story ... just another fireside fairy tale. Nothing seemed clear to Moncha. All was confusion and darkness.

Moncha rolled toward the fire and looked at Locke.[23] He was still sleeping. She decided to slip away to get the water so he would not get angry at her when he awoke. She always went to the spring when she was sure she would not meet anyone else there. She could not bear the weight of their condemning glances.

She took her bucket and crept through the woods to the spring. The bleak light of early morning made the sky grow gray. The trees were dark, and there were no leaves budding, even though it should be spring. Moncha felt as dead as the land. There was no fruit in her life. The man she was with did not love her; none of them ever had.

As she walked, she thought of how she had ended up with Locke, hiding out in an abandoned, crumbling dwelling house. She had been barely three years old when her parents had left her with her aunt and uncle. They had never returned. She was abandoned. She had known she was unwanted while growing up and was often reminded that she could be thrown out at any time. Images of her lonely, unhappy childhood came through her mind; bitter reminders that she was worthless and unlovable.

She remembered the night she came home without the money her aunt and uncle expected from her daily job of carrying water for a woman, a widow who brewed ale.

She had been only six, and it was very difficult for her to carry the heavy buckets over and over again. Sometimes, she was not sure what would give out first, her arms or her legs. That day, while she carried what must have been the eleventh or twelfth bucket, she had stumbled over a large stone that was hidden from view. She fell, scraping her leg so badly that the blood dripped down toward her ankle. She hobbled back home to get bandaged up.

"What are you doing here?" yelled her aunt, in her shrill voice. Her eyes were piercing as she stood up from scrubbing clothes in the washtub in front of the one-room dwelling house they all shared. "Why aren't you at work, Moncha?" The way she pronounced Moncha's name always made it sound as if she was cursing, spitting it out as an insult.

Moncha didn't dare say a word as her aunt towered above her, but she moved her hand revealing her bloody wound, and showed her aunt.

"What? Well, that's nothing. Nothing at all! You came back here for that? She'll never pay you your day's wages now! Huh! I do you the favor of taking you in and putting a roof over your head and I ask so little of you ... but you! You think you are some kind of princess or something, and you don't have to work like everyone else? Well, go on; I don't want to look at you." With that, her aunt turned her back and started her work again.

Moncha stood there for a moment, not sure what to do. Then she hobbled down to the spring and washed her leg. The cool water soothed the burning pain. She tore the bottom of her skirt to make a bandage for the wound, and bit her lip to try to stop herself from crying. "You are so ungrateful, Moncha! Why don't you ever do anything right?" Then she left the spring, limping back to start her chores.

Even now, walking in the bleak light toward the spring so many years later, Moncha still bore the scars of that fall. She shook off the memory as she slid her hand down to the pocket of her skirt. Her fingers found the opening and reached inside to feel a cool, smooth mirror. It was her only real possession. She had gotten it as a present the day she was born. It was the only tangible thing that connected her to her past. She brought out the mirror and, though it was dark, she could make out her image. She was dirty. Her face was as shameful as always. She was wicked, through and through, just like they had always told her. Worthless. Unlovable. Rejected.

"Why can't I be good enough? Why can't I be what they want? I try so hard but it does no good." A lone tear ran down her cheek. She had long since lost the ability to really cry. Her heart had been broken for such a long time that her tears were all but dried up.

When she got to the spring, she thought, "Perhaps I should end it all. Perhaps I should go far away where no one will ever find me. Perhaps I should find the Great and Terrible Dragon and, if he is merciful at all, he will kill me and put an end to this terrible life of mine."

Moncha was so deep in her thoughts that it took her a moment to see the light hitting her muddy boots. She stopped, frozen with fear, as she sensed the presence of another. She took a breath and slowly tipped her head up so she could see where the light was coming from. In front of her was a beautiful woman. Her skin glowed like shining bronze. Her long black hair cascaded down her back with streaks of white flowing like ribbons throughout it. Her face was lovely, and her smile warm and confident. She wore a dazzling white gown that touched the muddy forest floor. All about her seemed light.[24] Her eyes were bright and sparkling, and yet there was an uncomfortable intensity in them as she looked at Moncha.

Moncha was speechless. Her mouth fell open and she wondered if she was dead.

4

"Good morning, favored one," the apparition spoke.

Favored one? She must have the wrong person, Moncha thought to herself.

"I am Saoirse[25] and I have been sent to tell you about my Lord, the King of Glory."[26]

Moncha gasped. No one spoke that name in the Dominion of Darkness. "The King of Glory" is what the faithful had called the One and Only of the legend.

"Moncha, he has been calling you,[27] he wants you to know him.[28]... He wants you to join him in the Kingdom of Light."[29] Her voice was smooth and rich, reminding Moncha of silken fabric, and her face shone like a warm fire.

Moncha looked around, afraid someone might see her speaking to this ... what did she say her name was? Saoirse? How did she know Moncha's name?

"What are you? Are you going to kill me?"

"I am a child of the Almighty One, a citizen of the Kingdom of Light. I belong with him and, little one," she smiled warmly, "you belong with him, too." Moncha felt terror seeping into her body; her breath came faster.

"If you are really from the Kingdom of Light, you must go! You must! They hate you here; they will kill us both," Moncha said while motioning with her hands for the vision to leave.

"But I had to come, little one. Don't you remember me?"

Moncha looked at the woman. Remember her? Surely she would remember having met an apparition before.

"I was Mara;[30] you were my water girl when I brewed ale to sell in the tavern."

Moncha felt as if her whole world was spinning; memories flooded her mind. This woman, Mara, yes ... yes, she did remember Mara. It had been so long ago ... the memories started to sharpen in her mind as her eyes searched the ground. She could picture Mara. She was the widow Moncha had worked for when she was only six years old, the one she had just been thinking about on the way to the spring!

She remembered now; Mara had lost her husband and her sons to the war. She had been so bitter, so hateful. She, like many poor women, brewed ale to support herself, and she hired Moncha to get her the water she needed. If Moncha had spilled even a little of the water from the bucket on one of her many trips, Mara would not pay her anything for the day. If she came home without money, her relatives would berate her for being so wicked, assuming she had kept the money for herself. She would be forced to sleep outside for the night. Mara? Moncha looked up suddenly.

"This can't be … you can't be Mara? You can't be!" Moncha exclaimed.

"Little one," she looked at Moncha with a gentle smile and compassionate eyes, "I am. Our time is short, but I wanted to say," she sighed, and her sparkling eyes began to tear, "I am sorry I treated you so horribly. I want to ask you to forgive me."

Moncha was confused and upset. What if Locke woke up and came looking for her? What if someone else discovered them? She searched her mind for understanding. How could she make Mara – or Saoirse – go away?

"What does 'forgive' mean? What do you want from me?" she said, her face wrinkled with frustration.

Mara's tears increased as her heart overflowed with compassion for Moncha.

"I am sorry; you don't understand forgiveness, do you? No one ever forgives here," she sighed, her eyes looking off into the distance. She seemed to gather her thoughts and continued, "Forgiveness means that, even though what I did was wrong and ought not to have been done, you will not hold it against me or make me pay for it in any way; that you will … that you will be generous and let it go."[31]

Moncha was confused. What could she possibly have to offer this woman?

6

"I would like to give you forgiveness, but I am not sure I have it," Moncha said softly. She was angry at herself for failing to help the woman. Why was she always so wicked? So wicked, wicked, wicked…

"Moncha, don't be discouraged, that is not the only reason I am here," Saoirse said, interrupting Moncha's thoughts. Moncha looked up and saw that she had regained her former confidence and brilliance. "The Almighty One sent me here. Moncha, the Legend … it is true. The King of Glory lives! He is the ruler of the Kingdom of Light. His father, the Almighty One, gave it all to him. It is the most wonderful place, and he wants us all to join him there! It is just beyond the mountains," she said, motioning toward the peaks in the distance. "He wants you, Moncha, *you* to join him there."

Moncha took a couple of steps back, away from Saoirse. This was all too much to take in.

"What??? How???"

"He will come for you, and when he does, you must put your trust in him.[32] He defeated the dragon; it didn't seem like he did, but he did. When he died, Moncha, when he died, the power the dragon had over us, the power that wickedness itself had over us … was broken!"[33] She turned and took Moncha's hand, "If you come, you will learn what forgiveness means. Oh, Moncha, you can leave the Dominion of Darkness. I have done it! The King of Glory rescued me and brought me into the Kingdom of Light! He wants to do it for you, too."[34] Then, Saoirse put her warm fingers under Moncha's chin, drawing Mocha's eyes up to look into her own. "He loves you. He wants you to come to the Kingdom of Light, but you must trust him. Please, you must believe that he has defeated the dragon and made a way for you to come."

"How can this be?" Moncha asked, pulling her face away and looking at the ground again.

"Wickedness ruled us all. We were slaves of the dragon and enemies of the King. We had sold ourselves to the dragon out of greed, out of fear ... he deceived us all." Her voice was grave, but then she began to sound hopeful again. "But when the One and Only, when the King of Glory offered himself to die, he paid the debt we owed for our wickedness. And when he came to life again, he broke the power of the dragon and of wickedness over us.[35] It's all too much to explain now. I must go. I do not want to put you in danger, and the hour is getting too late for us to talk more. Please, Moncha, please, I ask you," Saoirse took Moncha's hand in hers and looked compassionately into her eyes, "Be alert, and look for the One and Only, the King of Glory, and when you find him, put your trust in him to rescue you like he rescued me." Then, Saoirse kissed Moncha's hand, released it and began walking away.

Moncha watched as she drifted into the misty distance, glowing in the grey light of the morning. After a while, she was no longer visible. Moncha bent down and put her pail under the spring. She was shaking.

Part of her wanted to believe Mara's words more than anything. She was so beautiful now, so free. Moncha wanted to understand what it meant to forgive. She wanted to see the Kingdom of Light, but it seemed so far away. Was that whole conversation real or had she imagined it? Could the Mara she remembered really have been transformed into the beautiful, hopeful, loving woman, Saoirse? She longed to believe it was true, but when she looked around at the shadowy woods around her, it seemed like foolishness.[36] Still, she could not let it go. A little seed had grabbed hold inside her and was beginning to take root. As she walked back with the water, she pondered these things in her heart.

CHAPTER II

It was a dark and wet night. There was some meager light afforded by the full moon as it struggled to penetrate the fog and gloom of the Dominion of Darkness. Locke had forced Moncha from the warmth of the fire until she came back with some water to cook for his friends. Smarting from his cutting words and a reckless shove, she was now feeling her way through the dangerous, dark forest. She felt as if the trees were moving to stand in her way, and every shadow was hissing at her to go no farther, yet she pressed on. She had no choice.

As she neared the spring, she recalled the day she had seen Saoirse. It was just a year ago, but it seemed like an eternity. Moncha had all but convinced herself it had been a fantasy. She had never spoken of it to anyone. She had played with the memory in her thoughts, like one special jewel in a lifetime of rejection and shame.

"What if it had happened? What if Saoirse really had been rescued from this place? What if she was free? And what if someone – someone big and powerful and good – really did know about her? What if he was merciful? What if he…" She stopped walking, and her eyes searched the dark sky as she whispered, "What if … he loves me?"

Her voice didn't seem to penetrate the gloom around her, and she began moving her weary feet again. Her life had not changed much since she had met Saoirse. She had tried for a while to be "good," but had failed again, falling back into old patterns. Things seemed about as hopeless today as they had the day she had met Saoirse; when she wondered why she could never change, could never be what people wanted. She took the mirror out of her pocket and, even though it was dark, she could make out the same image she had always seen. She saw her wicked, worthless and shameful face. She sighed, put it away and continued on.

She arrived at the area surrounding the spring. It was muddy from the rains of the day. Why Locke insisted on having water from the spring when they could have caught rain water, Moncha did not know and did not dare ask. She crouched down to fill her bucket as she had done for as many years as she could remember. It had always been her job to fetch the water. She despised it.

"Could you get me a drink, too, please?"[37]

Moncha looked up with a gasp and dropped her bucket, her heart pounding in her chest. It was a man's voice, and here she was, unprotected and alone with him in the dark. She was gripped with terror as she turned to face him. But when she saw him, her fear turned to wonder and curiosity. He was different from the men she knew. She couldn't explain how. It wasn't his clothes, or his height,[38] but there was something peculiar about him. Maybe it was his eyes. His eyes seemed to shine with something. Something kind and light.

He smiled as he repeated himself, "Will you give me a drink?"

"You sir, ask me for a drink?" Moncha could not understand why such a man would ask her for a drink … and she worried that, if he really knew who she was, he would not want to associate with her. "Sir, you do not know who I am; if you did, you would not want to speak with me." She turned to retrieve her bucket.

"Oh, Moncha, I know exactly who you are."

Moncha's eyes grew wide, and her pail clattered to the ground. Fear gripped her heart again, and her breath came fast. She turned back around.

"You … you know my name?"

"I know that you are Moncha, born of Eloise and Lorne. Your parents left you with your aunt and uncle when you were very young. They never came back for you."

Moncha's eyes grew wide with wonder and fear.

"I know that the first thing you stole was your grandmother's necklace, which you sold to a traveling merchant. With it you bought passage to the next village. There, you indulged your every whim and married your first husband. He left you just a few years later." The man's voice was gentle, but the words cut Moncha, and her heart began to ache. "You have had many men in your life since then,[39] much stealing, lying and many, many loves. The man you are with now is not your husband."

Moncha stood, her arms empty at her sides, stunned. Her mouth hung wide open, and she did not know how to respond. She felt uncovered before the man who knew everything she had ever done.[40] Who was he? And then, in her heart, the seed that had been planted by Saoirse sprouted within her, and she cried out, "You are the King of Glory!"

He smiled.

"Yes, dear one, I am. I have come to rescue you, that you might have hope and life. I have come to deliver you from the Dominion of Darkness and bring you into my Kingdom.[41] Will you come with me?"

"Saoirse," Moncha gasped, her mind reeling. "Saoirse came. She told me about you. She was … changed. I could tell. I could see it in her eyes. She was beautiful, but it was

11

more, she was…" Moncha searched her mind for the words, "…free somehow."[42]

"Yes."

"It made me think that maybe the King of Glory was more than a myth."

"I am,"[43] he said.

And she looked up into his eyes and said, "My Lord, it is you!" And she threw herself at his feet. He knelt down and wiped the teardrops from her eyes and kissed her forehead.

"It is good to hear you call my name, Dear One. Come with me; this is not where you belong. Come, and I will bring you to my Kingdom, the Kingdom of Light."

"Really?" she looked down at her filthy clothes and felt her shame, "You would want me there?"

"Of course. I have made a place for you." He brought his face close to hers and lowered his voice. "I have longed to be gracious to you; I have come now to show you my compassion. Please let me do so,"[44] he said, rising to his full height and pulling her up by her hand.

The loveliest and most comforting sensation was flowing into her heart. She thought, "Maybe this is what hope feels like," as she covered her heart with her hand and looked into the King of Glory's eyes.

"I offer you forgiveness for all of your selfish and rebellious deeds and all your wrongdoing. I also offer freedom from the power of wickedness so you do not have to continue in these evil paths any longer. I offer to bring you into my Kingdom and to deliver you into a new life[45]… if you believe that I am the Lord, as you called me, and that the Almighty One indeed raised me from the dead, as the legend teaches, you need only to receive the gift[46] that I offer you freely and to admit your need for forgiveness and deliverance from this life."

Moncha was not sure she understood all that he offered or what forgiveness really was, but she wanted desperately to leave her horrid, dark life. Since she had seen Saoirse, the hunger to experience the new life Saoirse possessed had steadily grown within her. She wasn't sure what it all meant, but she knew that she wanted it.

"I am sorry, so sorry, for all the wicked things I have done ... and I have surely noticed I have been powerless to be better, no matter how hard I try." Moncha said, thinking of her hopeless past. "Please ... forgive me ... and give me this gift. I would love a chance at a new life."[47] She finished quietly, then looked away from him and at her feet instead, a bit scared.

He let go of her hand and mounted his horse. He spoke with great authority, "Do not be afraid, Moncha. I am the Living One; I was dead, and see now that I am alive for ever and ever!" His voice softened to its former tone, "Come, come with me to my Kingdom." [48]

CHAPTER III

She wasn't sure just where the faith came from – it was like a gift[49] dropped right into her heart. She trusted him in that moment and she took his hand. Immediately she was mounted on the horse behind him, and they were galloping along the dark paths of the Dominion of Darkness. She was surprised to find that even the darkness seemed full of light[50] as she rode with the King of Glory.

Her mind was reeling. How could this be? How could someone so powerful and important have come to rescue her? And he knew what she had done! He knew what kind of woman she was.[51] She marveled at it all as she held close to her savior.

She felt that she could ride on and on forever. Nothing was wrong when she held close to him. Nothing could harm her.[52] Branches whisked past her. The air was getting cooler as the night wore on. She turned her face and watched the stars. They seemed brighter than they had ever been before.

She was now farther from her home than she had ever traveled. The forest was opening up into hilly passages in the foothills of the mountains. She had always heard that the mythical Kingdom of Light was beyond the mountains. Now, she would find out for herself!

As they rode on, she heard a sound, something she could not make out at first, but she felt the chest of the King of Glory vibrating beneath her arms. Then she heard it at last. He was singing! He was singing a song about a girl, a girl named "Kamea."[53] And, as she heard the song, a thrill went through her. She knew she was the one he was singing about.

Just then, he turned his head around and said, "Your new name, your true name, is Kamea. That is what I have always called you, and always will." He turned back around and resumed his song, his rejoicing[54] song[55] of saving his dear, darling Kamea.

Kamea hardly dared to believe that all this was real. She felt she must be dreaming, or that this was a joke, and he would soon cast her down to the ground where she belonged. But the horse did not slow and his song did not wane as they rode through the curvy paths cut into the mountains.

Her heart was bursting with joy from all that was happening to her. They had been riding all night, and yet she did not feel tired. She did not dare stop to blink in fear that everything might fade away!

"Kamea" was the song that played in her heart. As the birds began to call forth the morning, she felt even they were singing her new name in their songs. The King and Kamea had breached the summits of the mountains, and Kamea was surprised by the horse suddenly stopping at the edge of a cliff. She held tightly to the One and Only, her savior, so as not to fall off.

"Behold the Kingdom of Light!" the King of Glory announced as they suddenly were over the summit and saw the land flooded with brilliant, warm light

Everything before her was as perfect as a dream. There were no shadows, only light. The land was fruitful and fragrant as it spread out before them. In the midst of it was a lone mountain, and perched atop the mountain was a castle that was so large it extended beyond her ability to see.

"That is where we are going," the King said. "There is a place prepared for you." Then he nudged the horse and they were off.

The descent to the castle was thrilling. The horse and rider were both experts at navigating the steep slopes, even with the extra rider along. Kamea alternated between being terrified and exhilarated. If this was a dream, it was the best dream of her life, and she wanted to remember it all to ponder in the dull, dark days to come.

All at once, dread came over her. What would happen now? She looked down at her dirty clothes. What would the others think of her in this land? Were they used to people coming from the Dominion of Darkness? Had others come? Might she see Saoirse here so that she could thank her? She had so many questions as they raced across the level fields. She saw many beautiful and powerful animals awaken as they rode by. There were flowers everywhere, and the smell was sweet. Just ahead of them, there was a bed of sunflowers that were opened to the brilliant light around them, and just beyond the sunflowers was the enormous castle.

"I hope his father is as kind as he is," Kamea thought to herself.

A gate appeared ahead of them. As they neared it, she saw that it was white and seemed to glow brilliantly. The King of Glory did not slow the horse's pace as they neared the obstacle, and she was about to cry out when the doors were flung open before them. As they raced through, she heard echoing behind them, "Open up the doors that the King of Glory may come in!"[56]

She looked around the courtyard and saw many people all dressed in brilliant white,[57] as Saoirse had been. Kamea noticed there were people from every tribe of the world.

16

They were beautiful, for their faces shone; they were all radiant.[58]

They all looked at her confidently and with a sweet contentment about them. They did not seem alarmed at her arrival, or surprised at her appearance.

Still, Kamea wished she could hide.[59] She was ashamed to be so wicked and dirty before such perfect people. She felt angry to have to be among them this way. She felt an accusation form in her heart, "Did you bring me here only to humiliate me?"

But as the King of Glory turned to face her, it all melted away. He had such a look of love in his eyes. He jumped down and held out his hand to help her down. Her legs were weary after such a long ride, and she suddenly realized she was very tired. He seemed to sense this and caught her up in his arms.[60]

She turned her face to him and smiled a weak smile, "Thank you," she said quietly. Before she could stop herself, she had fallen asleep.

CHAPTER IV

"Good morning, Kamea, and welcome to the Kingdom of Light."

Kamea heard the voice and opened her eyes. She found herself in a stunning bedroom with light streaming in through large glass windows made of leaded panes. The whole room glowed with golden light. Kamea was warm and comfortable, in a large bed with a canopy and soft, silken covers. She had the loveliest feeling, and realized that, for the first time she could remember, she had not had any nightmares at all. She sat up in the bed with sweet contentment soothing her mind. Then she realized someone had spoken to her and she turned to see a man, dressed in white, standing before her. She also noticed a young woman putting a silver tray on the table on the patio.

"Good morning, Kamea. I am so glad to meet you."

"Yes, thank you, I am so happy to meet you. ..." Kamea answered politely, but she was a bit confused. "Excuse me, but I don't know who you are or why you are in my room. ... Where is the King of Glory?" she asked hesitantly.

"He had to go away, but he sent me here to you. I am your Counselor. [61] I am here to guide you into an understanding of the truth."[62] He saw Kamea's puzzled

18

expression and continued. "You have been living in the Dominion of Darkness your entire life, and it is a place where lies are exalted.[63] It will take you time to learn the realities of the King of Glory, the Almighty One, the Kingdom of Light, and even yourself."

Kamea wondered at what he was saying.

"I am here to reveal the things of the Kingdom to you and to teach you," he continued. "It is a great honor and my great delight. We are all so overjoyed that you are here with us. We rejoice that another daughter of the King is where she belongs."

The young woman turned from her work preparing the tea, and smiled in agreement.

Kamea had slipped over to the edge of the bed and put her feet on the floor. She noticed a pair of cozy slippers and longed to try them on, but was afraid that to do so would be too forward. The Counselor seemed to sense what she was thinking and said,

"Go ahead and try on the slippers. All of the blessings of the Kingdom are yours; they have been richly provided for your enjoyment![64] The Almighty One delights in giving good gifts[65] of all kinds to his children. Oh, and with that we will begin your first lesson."

Kamea was sliding her feet into the slippers and looked up as he caught her eye.

"Your first lesson is that you are a child [66] of the Almighty One."

Kamea considered this as she cautiously walked over to the small table on the patio where some tasty food was sitting on a silver tray. She wasn't sure what he could possibly mean, and her stomach was growling.

"Could we do this first lesson while I eat breakfast? I find I am quite hungry." And she smiled. Kamea could not remember smiling so much in all her life.

"Certainly, that is a great idea. Thank you, Adelaide,"[67] He said, nodding to the young woman. She bowed to both the Counselor and Kamea, and left. Kamea and the

Counselor were seated as she started in on the breads, cheeses and fruits. Strawberries had always been her favorite; she used to gather them for her aunt, and she always ate as many as her stomach could hold before returning home. There were also some fruits here she had never tasted or seen before, and each one had its own unique and delicious flavor. And the view from the patio was amazing! Kamea could see the citizens of the Kingdom of Light going to and fro throughout the castle grounds.

"Now, then, Kamea," the Counselor said, breaking her out of her fascination with breakfast and the view, "many things occurred when you accepted the King of Glory's offer and trusted him to save you. You have been rescued from the Dominion of Darkness, and you have been brought into the kingdom of the One and Only. It is much more than just moving from one land to another…" He took a deep breath and looked at her with smiling eyes, "You have been transformed.[68] Really, so many things happened, and a lot of them are not immediately perceived, so it will take some time for you to understand them. I would like to ask you to agree to be patient and to trust this one overwhelming principle: The Almighty One loves you. Please, will you just repeat that for me out of your own mouth?"

Kamea felt foolish and embarrassed to do such a thing, but she did not want to anger the Counselor on her first day in the Kingdom of Light. So, she swallowed her bit of cheese and then spoke softly, "The Almighty One loves me." She felt her cheeks blush.

"Yes," The Counselor looked her in the eye, "Yes he does. He loves you so much that he did not spare his only son misery on your account."[69]

"The One and Only?"

"Yes, the King of Glory. You see, all of the people of the Dominion of Darkness have broken an ancient law. They have chosen wickedness over goodness. Not one of them consistently does what is right. [70] Everyone does whatever they feel like doing, without regard for the ancient law or the Almighty One – often without regard even for other people. They follow the path of their choosing and of their desires,[71] not the path of goodness, the path of the One and Only."

"Well, I think some try…" Kamea said weakly. She had thought of how she had tried to do good after meeting Saoirse. It had been difficult and it all seemed hopeless.

"That may be, but trying is not enough, is it?"[72] He looked softly at Kamea, "No one can escape the Dominion of Darkness and move into the Kingdom of Light by themselves. There is only one way to get here.[73]"

"By accepting the offer of the One and Only…" Kamea said, her thoughts coming together.

"That's right, Kamea. That's right. But, as I said before, more has happened to you than is apparent now. You have been rescued not only from the land of darkness, but also from the dominion, from the power and rule, of evil. You've been a prisoner to wickedness your whole life, but now … now you've been delivered from that into freedom."[74]

"Like Saoirse," Kamea said wistfully, remembering the liberty she sensed when she met Saoirse by the spring a year ago.

"Yes, like Saoirse," the Counselor said smiling, but then his face and voice became more serious. "But there was a price that had to be paid to offer you this gift. Every person in the Dominion of Darkness had broken the ancient law when they turned away from the Almighty One and disobeyed him. And the penalty for the guilt of each person in the Dominion of Darkness, the price[75] demanded by justice, is death."

"Death!" Kamea exclaimed. It seemed ridiculous until she considered it some more. What should be the price of all the wicked, evil things she had done…and those that had been done to her? What should it cost?

21

"Yes, Kamea, the price that needed to be paid to make a way for you to come here was death. But you did not have to pay it."

Suddenly Kamea's mind started putting it all together. "The One and Only, he … he died in the storm after he fought the dragon…"

"Yes, Kamea, The Almighty One did not hold back his son, the One and Only; but he gave him up to be tortured and he died in your place so that you would not have to be separated from the King anymore, so that you wouldn't have to live in the Dominion of Darkness anymore, but instead you could have everlasting life here in the Kingdom of Light. And the King of Glory loves you very much, so much that he chose to suffer in order to save you."

Kamea was not completely comfortable with these ideas. She was incredibly grateful to be delivered from the Dominion of Darkness and was ecstatic to be enjoying the good things in this Kingdom, but she didn't like having caused someone so much trouble. She also wondered what the King would want in return. She didn't want to bring these things up to her Counselor, so she continued to eat and poured herself some tea. "Would you like some tea?"

"Yes, please," the Counselor said, smiling. Kamea could get used to having people smile at her. It was so foreign to her, and yet so welcome.

He continued as Kamea again found her seat and started buttering another piece of bread.

"So, the first lesson is that, even though the cost was dear, the Almighty One was pleased to adopt you as his daughter and to make you a co-heir with his son."

The butter knife fell from her hand, and her full mouth hung open. "What … What do you mean?"

"You are the Almighty One's adopted daughter. You are in the King of Glory's family, and a co-heir."[76]

Kamea's face expressed her concern as her mind tried to grasp that she was a daughter to the King, "But if I'm a daughter to a king, I'm a —"

"Princess."

"No. I can't be," Kamea searched the Counselor's face to see if he were teasing her but there was no mock in his expression. He simply sat back and took a sip of his tea.

"Yes, you are a princess, a member of the royal family."

"But how? Why?"

"He chose you. He chose you because it pleased him to do so.[77] You are his child because he loves you.[78] You are precious and honored in his sight.[79]"

Kamea was surprised to find a smile coming to her lips and a giggle escaping.

"A daughter and an heir? But I'm such a nobody. No one ever … ever wanted me." Kamea thought over her life, and this just didn't fit. And yet, it was such a lovely thought. She turned and looked out at the Kingdom. It was all hers. She was a co-heir.

"So, when the Almighty One dies, I will inherit all this?"

"Not exactly. When *you* die, you will inherit[80] the entire Kingdom, along with the other adopted children of the Almighty One. There is even more to the Kingdom than can be revealed to you at this time."

"I inherit the Kingdom when *I* die? Hmmm." Kamea threw this idea to the back of her mind. It was too big to grasp. The buttered bread melted in her mouth, and she spread butter on the next piece.

"So, in review, the Almighty One and his son both love you. You are the adopted daughter of the Almighty One and a co-heir with the son. The Almighty One has done this of his own choice, his own will, and he himself has qualified you[81] for this inheritance. So, what that means is you did not earn it,[82] it was a gift."

A gift.

Kamea thought about it. The Almighty One had done all this on her behalf and not because of anything she had done.[83] He had chosen to do it.

"The Almighty One must be all goodness and light," she said, almost to herself.

23

"Oh, he is. He is entirely good and there is no darkness in him at all.[84] He is the source of love[85] and life.[86] He is the most generous and the most merciful. I know this was a lot to take in today, but I want to share just a couple of other ideas with you that I think will be helpful as you live here."

Kamea straightened up in her seat, assuming that now she was going to hear the bad news, but there was only good news to be shared.

"You are a member of this household,[87] like all the others you saw when you came in yesterday. You are all children of the Almighty One."

Kamea wanted to belong and be able to remain, but she had so many questions. It all seemed too good to be true.

"So I can stay?"

"Yes, Kamea," the Counselor answered gently. "You can stay. We will discuss the privileges and responsibilities of being a member of our household some other time. Perhaps now we should go for a walk."

Kamea nodded in agreement as she continued to consume berries and cheese.

"I will leave you now so you can change into your new clothes."

The Counselor rose and began to walk toward the door, then paused.

"Oh, and one more thing…" He turned toward a tall, narrow piece of furniture that was covered with a long white cloth.

"You will notice there is only one piece of furniture covered in this room. It is a mirror. We find that those who have been recently rescued need time to adjust before looking in the mirror. Please leave it alone until I tell you it's time to remove the covering."

"Oh, all right," Kamea said, wondering why it would be hard to look in a mirror. The Counselor excused himself and quickly shut the door behind him. Kamea pondered what he had said about the mirror. It left a sick feeling in her stomach. She sat down on her bed and reached down into her skirt pocket. Her small mirror was still there. She pulled it out, feeling its familiar smooth, cool metal and its turnings. She turned it over and looked into it, hoping to see the changes she already felt inside of her.

She was dismayed.

Everything was the same as every other time she had looked into it. She was worthless and wicked, like always.

"He does not want me to see how wicked I am and that nothing at all has changed. That is why he does not want me looking into the large mirror."[88]

She sighed.

She had hoped. But hope had never worked before.

"Perhaps it will just take more time," she thought.

CHAPTER V

She poured some water from the pitcher into a basin and washed up. Then she walked over to the wardrobe to look for some clothes for the day. When she opened the door, she was amazed at the fine dresses, skirts, blouses and aprons inside. She also was surprised that everything was white. She had never before in her entire life worn white and she felt awkward about putting on such fine clothes. And yet, she didn't want to walk around this place in her old, dirty clothes. She longed to fit in here. She found the most simple skirt and blouse and added an apron to it. The clothes were soft, and she felt a sense of honor come over her as she put them on. She noticed some carvings along the inside of the wardrobe. She ran her fingers over them and read: "COMPASSION, KINDNESS, HUMILITY, GENTLENESS and PATIENCE."[89] Then, as she lifted out a pair of new boots from the floor of the wardrobe, she noticed this inscription: "THIS IS HOW THE KING'S CHOSEN AND DEARLY LOVED PEOPLE SHOULD CLOTHE THEMSELVES."

Kamea took a deep breath and sat down to put on her boots. It was all so much to take in. She wasn't sure what it all meant. As she slipped the boots on, she was amazed that they fit perfectly; they were practical, too. She felt ready[90] for anything. Even so, she decided to wait for the Counselor to return and found herself back at the breakfast table, eating what was left of the bread and butter.

Their walk revealed the incredible grounds around the castle. There were all kinds of animals, and garden after garden of lovely, fragrant flowers and luscious fruits and vegetables. The people of the Kingdom of Light each went about their work with a gentle intensity. Some were found singing praises of the King of Glory as they trimmed bushes and cut blooms to put on the banquet tables.

Kamea and the Counselor passed through a lovely, cavernous hallway where many people were working together, painting a massive mural, expressing their love and adoration to the King of Glory. With so many styles mixing and working together, it made a fantastic and dynamic work of art.

Kamea stood and looked at it for what seemed like hours. Her eyes longed to search out every stroke, to know the heart of each artist who had poured out praise and admiration of the King on the wall. The Counselor assured her they could return to see the progress on the mural another day, and they walked farther on. There were people dancing in a room down the hall. She was captivated with the coordination of movement among these people,[91] old and young, from so many different villages and provinces back in the Dominion of Darkness.

"This place, all that is done here, it is all so beautiful," Kamea said. Her heart was full of inspiration from witnessing the expressions of love and beauty all around her.

"Yes, let me show you some more."

The Counselor turned and they left the artists' hall. As they walked pass a group under a spreading tree Kamea asked, "What are they doing?"

"They are training to be Keepers of the Legend."

27

"The Keepers *are* from the Kingdom of Light!"

"Yes, Kamea. They were once in the Dominion of Darkness themselves, and now they are given the task to go back and share the Legend with others ... of course, we know the Legend is much more than a fireside tale, now, don't we?"

Kamea smiled in agreement. The Keepers of the Legend were sent out from the Kingdom of Light. Of course, it all made sense. As they continued their tour the Counselor walked Kamea past a small barn. They came to the back and saw a man cleaning up the hay and clearing out the manure. Kamea was shocked such a place existed here but, when she looked at the man, she saw his face shining.

"Truman, [92] how is your day going?" the Counselor asked him.

"Lovely. I am enjoying it very much. It is always a blessing to have useful and meaningful work to do."

"Thank you for your faithfulness, Truman," the Counselor replied. "This is Kamea. She is new here."

"Welcome, Kamea. It is great to have you among us."

Kamea offered a small, tight smile and a nod. She still wasn't sure what was expected of her here and she was uncomfortable in such a smelly place. It reminded her too much of her former life.

"Well, we won't keep you from your work," said the Counselor as he guided Kamea toward the path. They stopped just a short walk away and found a seat on some large rocks by a stream. They sat for a while, and Kamea drifted deep into thought.

"It doesn't seem fair," Kamea said, finally interrupting the silence as they watched the water flow by.

"What do you mean, Kamea?" the Counselor asked.

"I mean, why do so many people get to do such lovely things and Truman is stuck with such a lowly job? Did he displease the Almighty One?"

"No, he pleases the Almighty One very much. He is trusted with an important job, and Truman finds it satisfying to perform it faithfully.[93] Did it seem like he thought it was unfair?"

Kamea thought for a minute.

"No, I guess not." She kept thinking on this.

After a while, the Counselor invited her to begin walking with him again. They walked along the brook, and the Counselor continued his explanation.

"Everyone here has meaningful work to employ them. You will be assigned your service, too, when you are ready. It is a joy to do work in worship of the King of Glory."

They continued to walk and discussed many things about the Kingdom of Light. They walked a bit into the wood to a spring. Next to it, a bucket hung from a branch on a tree. A shiver went through her as she remembered her former life. She had no real specialized skills. She did not weave or make music. All she had ever done was fetch water and do chores around the house. She wanted to forget all of that now. The Counselor seemed to notice the change in her. "Would you like a drink?"

"No," Kamea said firmly. "No, I'm fine."

"And," she thought to herself, "I don't plan on touching one of those buckets ever again!"

CHAPTER VI

At dinner time, the Counselor told Kamea to get ready and then come down to join the others. He left her to go to her room to freshen up and gave her directions to the dining hall. Kamea paced in her room, fidgeting with her hands nervously. She was biting her lips, her habit when she was agitated. She started talking to herself, "I don't know, I don't know! How can I go down there with all those perfect people in their shining clothes? They are so…so pure in heart! You can see it in the joy and peace they have. I feel like…" she sighed and slid her hand down to touch the mirror in her pocket, "like an imposter."

She sat on the bed and gazed out the window for a while. Suddenly, an urge came over her to get out of there and get away. Before she knew it, she was out her door. She found her way through the ornate passages and majestic halls and went outside. In her haste, she had forgotten shoes, and she felt the cool earth under her feet. It was a familiar feeling; she had often gone without shoes when she was little. She began running away from the castle. It was twilight, and she could still make out her surroundings. She was running downhill and made it to a cluster of trees. She was out of breath as she sat down at the foot of a large pine tree, her back to the great castle.

As she rested there, tears started to fall from her eyes. Kamea was so upset; she did not even notice she was really crying for the first time in years.

"I don't belong here. I don't belong anywhere," she whimpered.

"Kamea, that is not true," rang a rich, gentle voice from the wood. She was startled, but immediately recognized the sound.

"Lord ... is that you?"

"Those who are mine," he said, emerging from the trees, his brilliance filling Kamea's hiding place, "those who belong to me know my voice."[94]

Kamea couldn't help herself; she got up and threw her arms around his neck and cried into his shoulder. He drew his strong and loving arms around her and held her. [95] Kamea could not remember ever being held so tenderly before. She remembered herself and pulled away from him. He loosened his grasp and looked into her eyes. "You are mine,[96] Kamea. This is where you belong."[97]

Kamea wanted to believe it so badly, but her mind was racing wildly. She could not accept this – it was all too good to be true.

For some reason at that moment, Kamea remembered the day she turned five years old...

She woke up early and rose from her blanket on the dirt floor of her aunt and uncle's home. She saw a brown paper package with a flower tied to it sitting on the table. Her heart jumped within her. Someone had remembered it was her birthday. She felt the ecstasy of such unexpected attention and walked over and reached for the package.

"What are you doing?"

The angry growl of her aunt's voice startled her.

"That is for my girl, Lamara.[98] What an ungrateful wretch you are, trying to steal from my daughter! I'll teach you a thing or two..."

31

and she shooed Moncha from the table with the end of a stick she used to stir the fire. Moncha ran from the house to escape. Her heart felt as if it would break. This was just one more lesson she was not favored, that she was not loved, that she was not cherished and that good gifts were never, ever going to be for her.

"Kamea," her thoughts were interrupted by the soft, strong voice again, pulling her out of her memory. "Kamea, I know that people have hurt you. They have said all kinds of things about you…but they are not right. I am the One you should listen to. My voice is the voice of truth.[99] You are protected now. I keep those who belong to me safe."[100]

Kamea wanted to believe him, but the hurt was too great. Then he shocked her.

"Kamea, on your fifth birthday, you awoke to find a gift," he said, "but your aunt said it was not for you."

Kamea's mouth dropped, and tears filled her eyes.

"I am so sorry that she hurt you like that. I do not desire that my little ones would be hurt in that way. But Kamea, do you remember the rest of the day? Do you remember what happened later on that day?"

Kamea felt confused and then, slowly, a dusty old memory came back.

"Yes, I think I remember…After my aunt chased me from the house, I went down to get water, as I always did, and there was a single crocus bloom there. I remember that I squatted down and just gazed at it. It was so beautiful, so delicate. It was white and perfectly clean. I … I delighted in that little flower." Kamea marveled at the memory. It was precious, and yet she had seldom thought of it in all the years since then.

"I gave you that gift,[101] Kamea. I remembered you."

Kamea looked up at him, startled.

"You have always been precious[102] to me, and I know everything that has happened to you.[103] I have kept a record of your tears;[104] I have numbered the hairs on your head.[105] You matter to me. Kamea, I love you, and you belong here.

32

Soon, you will visit my father, the Almighty One, and he will explain more to you."

He took a deep breath and looked around with lively eyes. "Will you join the others now?"

Kamea felt nervous about going back; by this time she would be late. She didn't want to go, but she very much wanted to please the King of Glory.

"Yes, I will go."

She turned to walk away but her heart hurt within her. She turned back and said, "But I want to stay with you!"

The King of Glory's face erupted into a beautiful smile. Kamea felt the delight[106] of it throughout her whole being.

"I am so glad that you would choose to spend time with me. It is good and right for you to want to be with me. I think that tomorrow afternoon we should go for a walk. Come here and meet me when the afternoon begins to cool."

"Should I tell my Counselor?" Kamea asked eagerly.

"He will know."

Kamea wondered at this response, but decided to let it go. She turned to walk back to the castle, and then turned back and ran to the King of Glory and hugged him. He hugged her back, then she ran back toward the castle. She felt like a child again. To have someone who did not reject her affection was wonderful. As she entered the castle, her heart felt so light and alive, she thought she just might fly away.

CHAPTER VII

Kamea reached the door of the dining hall. As far as she could see, people were sitting down at tables together. The tables were set for a feast, and conversation filled the air. There was a pleasant loudness to the whole setting and, above it all, some stringed instruments played a lively song. Everything was always light and brightness here, but this room seemed to have a special glow as so many of the citizens of the Kingdom of Light were gathered in one place. With so many people and so many tables, Kamea didn't know where to start looking for a place to sit. Overwhelmed, she took a step back toward the passageway. Then, she heard her Counselor right behind her saying,[107]

"Don't give up now; look over there, on the left. Saoirse is waiting for you."

"Oh," Kamea said, startled at his voice, but when she looked to the left, there Saoirse was. Saoirse looked up and caught Kamea's gaze. Her face warmed and she got up and hurried toward Kamea, obviously glad to see her.

"Kamea, my friend — my sister,[108] I am so glad you are here!" Saoirse said taking both of Kamea's hands in her own.

"Saoirse, it is so good to see you. I was hoping I would meet up with you here. Thank you for coming for me in…." she looked about nervously, not sure she should mention the Dominion of Darkness in a place as glorious as this.

"Oh, it was all joy, dear one. It was all joy. We are celebrating you and the other new arrivals tonight!" Saoirse said, a brilliant smile upon her face.

"Other new arrivals?"

"Yes. The King of Glory is passionate about gathering up his people, and he is constantly pursuing lost ones[109] in the Dominion of Darkness to bring them into his Kingdom. He loves us all so passionately. He doesn't want anyone to continue in despair and darkness."[110]

"No, I know that is true," Kamea reflected, "He loves us all so." Saoirse took a deep breath and looked at Kamea.

"Yes, dear Kamea, and I am filled with joy that you have come to know his love for yourself."

She took Kamea by one hand and led her through the maze of tables to a place where people had made room for her. As she sat down she was warmly welcomed by more radiant faces. Kamea was pondering what Saoirse had said about there being other newcomers. It comforted her to know she wasn't the only one who didn't know the customs of this new land; that she wasn't the only one adjusting to this new life.

People asked her about her day and they spoke of the King of Glory with love. Some discussed their work with joy and satisfaction. One of those near her was a Keeper of the Legend named Rawiya.[111] She had just returned after a month in the Dominion of Darkness, sharing the story of the One and Only with folks in fire-lit rooms. Her love for those people was eclipsed only by her adoration of the King of Glory.

"He rescued me when I was so lost. I don't know what I would have done if he had not come for me!"

Adelaide came and found a seat near Kamea and introduced herself.

"Hi, I'm Adelaide. I saw you this morning. ..."

"Yes, thank you for the tea and the food. I think I ate an entire loaf of bread myself!"

"Oh, I am so glad you enjoyed it. I will be sure to let the bakers know!" Adelaide answered with her characteristic humility and gentleness. Kamea immediately liked her.

The conversations continued and they all enjoyed the good food and laughed heartily as they shared stories, experiences and life together.

As Kamea later climbed the stairs to her room she felt a pleasant weariness. It had been such a good day. As she reached the door to her room the Counselor was there waiting for her. They opened the door, entered the room and sat down.

"I don't know when I have ever been so full!"

"The food was good tonight?"

"Yes!" and Kamea thought for a moment. "But it wasn't just the food, it was the companionship. I was so worried..."

Kamea stopped. She wasn't sure she wanted the Counselor to know everything she was thinking. She had learned over the years to keep her thoughts and feelings hidden so people wouldn't know her vulnerabilities. She was often embarrassed and ashamed of herself, so she spent most of her life hiding – afraid of being uncovered as the phony she knew deep down she was.

The Counselor looked at her with an open expression. She felt a longing to just open her heart to him, but she was stuck.

"Feeling stuck?" he asked.

Kamea looked at him in surprise.

"Kamea, I want you to know that you can trust me. I want the very best for you.[112] The King of Glory has sent me to you because he loves you and he wants me to comfort you and teach you and reveal things to you."[113]

Kamea wanted to believe him, but she still felt stuck.

"I should probably disclose something else to you."

Kamea felt her body tighten and her nerves bind in her stomach. Here it comes. Throughout her whole life there had always been a catch, and this was going to be no different. Her face was growing pale when the Counselor continued.

"What the father knows, he reveals to me…and he knows your heart. He knows all of your thoughts."

Kamea felt anxiety give birth to fear within her; this was not good news.

"If he knows all of my thoughts," Kamea thought to herself, "if that is really true, then I am in serious trouble."

"Now, I speak peace over you, child."

Kamea felt her body relax a little.

"I want you to understand this because the Almighty One knows all you have ever done, or even wanted to do.[114] He knows all that you have spoken, even before the words were on your tongue.[115] He knows all of this and he has still brought you here. He has still chosen you. You are safe. He isn't going to be disappointed or surprised when something about your life or your character is revealed. He already knows every weakness, every wicked deed and every fear of yours,[116] and he still wants you here."

He took a breath and looked calmly at Kamea.

"Just take that in and consider it."

Kamea sighed and relaxed a bit. These were big thoughts, but somehow she felt like she could grasp what he was saying. The Counselor's words were powerful and seemed to come with faith built into them. As she heard them, there was an assurance inside of her that they were true. Kamea wrestled with this in her mind. What if the King of Glory really did know how evil and rotten she could be, and still rode into the dangers of the Dominion of Darkness to save her?[117]

37

"Did he know all this about me when he fought the dragon?" Kamea suddenly blurted out. "Did he know all the awful things I would do?"

"All of the days of your life were laid out before him before one of them came to be.[118] He knows all things ... ALL THINGS. Nothing is hidden [119] from him." He softened his voice. "Yes Kamea, he knew."

"When he came for me he ... he mentioned me stealing..."

Her voice trailed off at the shame of it.

"Stealing your grandmother's necklace, the one from her wedding with the green gemstones in it? You sold it to a traveling merchant in the first village you entered and within two weeks you had wasted all the money."

"Yes," Kamea sighed. She accepted this was the truth about her. She was tired of trying to hide. "So, you know what the Almighty One and the King of Glory know?"

"Yes."

"And they know everything about me?"

"Yes."

"And they still," she took a deep breath. "They still wanted me here?"

"Yes, absolutely. You see, Kamea, there are no good people.[120] None. All have chosen wickedness. All need forgiveness. You have just begun your journey to understand the King of Glory. But," he looked intently into Kamea's eyes as his voice grew stronger, "I assure you, the King of Glory is all goodness and light.[121] His love is unfailing;[122] it is more powerful than death.[123] You are safe in his love. You belong here, simply because he desires you to be here, and that will not change. He is the same yesterday ... today ..." he smiled broadly as he finished, "... and forever."[124]

Kamea took in these last words, then felt the exhaustion of the day catch up with her.

"You need to sleep now. I will join you in the morning," the Counselor said, moving toward the open door.

Kamea got into bed, then remembered her conversation with the King. She weakly called to the Counselor, "Tomorrow, in the cool of the day…"

"You will be meeting the King of Glory for a walk."

Kamea remembered what the King of Glory had told her earlier; that the Counselor would "know." She was beginning to understand. He blew out the lights and left as Kamea melted into bed and was soon asleep.

CHAPTER VIII

The next morning was much like the first. She awoke as Adelaide was putting breakfast on the table on the patio. She smiled her usual friendly smile at Kamea.

"Oh goodness, Adelaide, do you know what time it is?"

"It's midmorning Kamea. I hope you like your bread this morning. The bakers were excited to give you one of their favorites!"

"Oh, thank them for me!" said Kamea in a hurry. Afraid the Counselor would be angry with her for being so lazy, she got up out of bed and dressed quickly. She had accidentally slept in her clothes, so she took a simple white dress from the wardrobe. As she walked across the room, the sheet over the mirror billowed from her passing. Kamea was tempted to take a peek and look in the mirror, but then decided not to. She reached her hand down to her pocket and pulled out her own mirror instead. The handle was worn from the years she had kept it with her at all times. So many times she had looked at the reflection, hoping to see a new likeness. Every time, she had been disappointed.

As she turned it over, the same old image reflected back at her. "How can this be?" her heart cried. She felt as if she had already changed so much. Or had she? Maybe she could not be changed. Maybe she would never be like people here. She wondered if anyone else had ever failed here before. She heard the door handle turn and quickly slid the mirror into her pocket. Turning to face the Counselor, Kamea put a big smile on her face and greeted him warmly, "Good morning!"

He looked at her with suspicion and then answered her, speaking his words slowly as he watched her closely, "Good morning, dear one. How are you doing?"

"I'm great," she said.

It was mostly true. She walked over to the table on the patio where the breakfast feast was laid out. "Join me?" They sat down as Adelaide slipped from the room unnoticed.

"Thank you, I don't need breakfast, but I would like to start another lesson while you eat."

"Certainly," she said, hoping he had forgotten his earlier suspicions.

It seemed he either had forgotten or decided not to pursue them.

"Yesterday we talked about how you are a member of the King of Glory's household, and a member of his family. A co-heir with the King of Glory and," he paused as he smiled at her, "that you belong."

"Yes, I remember, Counselor."

"Today, I want to share with you that you are also the King of Glory's friend."[125]

Kamea's brow furrowed as she spread jam on the fabulous brown bread Adelaide had brought her, and thought this over. "Isn't being family better than being a friend? Why would it matter if we were friends?"

"Well, consider it a moment and let me know your thoughts."

41

Kamea slowly chewed the bread. It was sweet and full of crunchy oats and nuts. She thought about family and friends. Her cousin Lamara was family, but she had always disliked Kamea. They had not been close. Once, when Kamea was quite young, she had tried to confide in Lamara about her fears, and Lamara had told everyone at dinner that night, making a big joke of it and humiliating Kamea in front of everyone. They were family, but not friends.

Then Kamea remembered she had made a friend when she first moved to a new village when her first marriage crumbled. She had met Alwine[126] in a tavern, and she had helped Kamea find a job getting water and doing the laundry for the manor house. They had worked together and laughed together, and it was one of the very few times in her life that Kamea had felt enjoyed by someone else. She put down her bread and sighed. "Friends are different than family."

"What do you think would be a difference?"

"You choose your friends, and they like you." Then Kamea thought for a second. "So does that mean that the King of Glory chose me as his friend?"

"I think you could definitely say that. There are some other things about your relationship to him that can not be defined by the kinds of friendships you have had. He is not like the people you have known. He is more loving, he is far more kind, and he is much more forgiving. He has made a way for you to be close to him. Have you ever hugged a king before you met the King of Glory?"

"Certainly not. I have never laid my eyes on any kings in the Dominion of Darkness. They are separate and far away from people like me."

"But the King of Glory has brought you near.[127] And you can approach him with confidence;[128] he will not turn you away."

Kamea thought of how she ran up to him the night before and hugged him. He certainly had not rejected her.

42

"Yeah," was all Kamea could say. Her bread was catching in her throat as it swelled with emotion, and she tried to wash it down with tea. As she drank it, she noticed the sweet flavor. It was just the right temperature, so she finished the whole cup. When she was done, she wiped her mouth with the back of her hand and sighed. When she remembered herself, she tried to regain her manners, "Oh, I'm sorry Counselor, I —"

"What, sorry?! Not at all. The Almighty One has given you everything richly to be enjoyed![129] I'm glad that you enjoyed your tea to that extent," he finished with a smile. Then he got up and pushed in his chair.

"Well, I think that is enough to think about for now. I will see you soon."

Kamea poured another cup of tea and held it close as she looked out across the wide valley below. It was all so beautiful, it seemed difficult to take it all in. It was as if her eyes could not fully contain so much brilliance and light. As she drank more tea, she felt something stir inside her. She felt a growing sense of something that had always evaded her before; at her every grasp, it had slipped away. Was she now, finally, going to have it for her very own? Was she home? And was this love?

CHAPTER IX

Kamea carefully got ready for her walk with the King of Glory. She was so excited, she went out to the pine trees long before the cool of the day to wait for him. She felt like she was a kid again. She waited in the shade and listened to leaves rustling in the distance. It was quite warm, and the feeling of the breeze on her face was like a soft caress. Before she knew what was happening, she felt a gentle nudge on her shoulder. She opened her eyes and realized she had fallen asleep. The King of Glory was on one knee and he was offering her a drink. She sat up, and he poured water into her mouth. Her eyes began to adjust to the brightness, and she felt uncomfortable.

"I must have fallen asleep."

"Yes, I imagine that is what happened," he said with his eyes smiling.

"I – I was afraid that you weren't going to come."

"You will learn that I always keep my promises. [130] Always," he said taking a seat next to her. "Well, why don't we sit here just a minute while you wake up, drink some water and recover from the heat of the day?"

"Oh, I do hope we will still get to take our walk." Kamea was afraid that she was wasting her limited time with the King of Glory and that he would have to go soon.

"We will take our walk."

He turned to face her. "Do you forget that I am king?" he smiled warmly at her.

Kamea did not want to admit that she did sometimes forget he was king. She felt uneasy.

"Why don't you take another drink and relax," he said. "I am glad that we can take this walk today. I have something to show you."

Kamea stood up and said, "I'm ready. Can we go now?" She was curious about what she would see.

The King of Glory took her hand [131]and led her on a trail through the evergreen trees. She rejoiced at their closeness and felt safe in the forest with him. She marveled at the height of the trees, and they discussed the wildlife and flowers they passed. All at once they came to the edge of a cliff, and the King of Glory put out his arm to guard Kamea from stepping over the edge. Her stomach felt queasy when she saw how far away the bottom of the chasm was.

The King of Glory looked gravely over the gulf into the distance. Kamea followed his gaze and saw lines of smoke. Then she heard shouting.

"What is that?"

"That is the sound of my enemies. They are fighting against our Kingdom."[132] He looked at Kamea with sad eyes.

"All those in the Dominion of Darkness, they are enemies of the Kingdom of Light." He looked back. "And of me."

"I know about this war," Kamea said softly, "When did it start?"

"Shortly after the beginning of the world People chose their own way... They chose to follow their cravings and

45

desires, to rebel against goodness and the authority of the Almighty One … They chose…"

And he looked over to the Dominion of Darkness.

"They chose this. They chose to be my enemy. All of them."

And then he turned to Kamea.

"Even you."[133]

Kamea was shocked. She looked at the battle going on across the chasm. "I didn't fight against you – I have never even used a sword!"

"But you were an enemy of goodness and light. You participated in dark deeds. You were selfish and worried only about yourself. You served your own stomach,[134] your own comfort, your own entertainment … You served yourself. And so," he turned to her, "you were my enemy.[135] We were separated. There was distance between you and me, as this chasm now separates us from that battle."

Kamea was uncomfortable. She looked at the deep, dark chasm and gulped.

"Why are you telling me this? I thought you wanted me here. Have you changed your mind?"

Kamea felt the old fear creeping back into her stomach, tightening the muscles in her back. She began biting her bottom lip.

The King of Glory took her hand as she was trying to back up.

"No. I am not like a mere man that I change my mind.[136] No. I am telling you this so you will understand. We were once enemies, but we are no longer enemies. When I fought the dragon, faced the storm and died, I paid the price that every person owed. Because you accepted my offer to pay the penalty of your evil deeds and words, and because I broke the power of evil over you, you and I are no longer enemies. There is peace between us.[137] The chasm has been removed, and we are now close."[138]

He punctuated this sentiment by lightly squeezing her hand in his. Then he turned to face the battle, his eyes becoming focused and severe.

"I am now, and will always be, angry at evil. Evil kills, steals and destroys.[139] It hurts the ones I love. There is no place in my kingdom for evil. But, all justice has been satisfied by my own death. Now ... now, we can have peace," he said as he looked at Kamea with gentle eyes.

"And so... your evil deeds have been paid for. You are no longer condemned. You are forgiven and at peace with me. I am telling you this so that you will understand that justice has been satisfied and mercy has been poured out. Now, you are forgiven.[140] Now you are cleansed and pure. And now, you are free from the power of evil:[141] You are free to do good deeds and turn from wicked ways."

Kamea tried to drink this all in. It was a sobering reality. She looked out at the battle. "Could they all make peace with you, too?"

"Yes," he said and he took a deep breath, tears forming in the corners of his eyes. "Yes, if they chose to trust me, as you did, and agreed that they need forgiveness."

"You would let those men; the ones who are hunting you down...who are battling against your kingdom ... you would let them in here?"

The One and Only turned to Kamea and put his hands on her shoulders. He looked compassionately into her eyes.

"Kamea, they are no different than you or any of the other citizens of the Kingdom of Light. I would certainly let them in. It is my passionate desire that they all would come."

He dropped his arms and turned and looked back at the battle across the chasm and spoke boldly. "I am the one who saves."[142]

Kamea looked away from the battle. This was an uncomfortable reality. She walked into the trees a bit and sat down on a stump facing some flowering trees. She felt quiet inside. Enemies. She had been an enemy of the King

47

of Glory.   She had been opposed to the great, compassionate, loving King of Glory.   She had been his foe. She felt the truth of it within her.

"Kamea, my dear one."

She turned to look into the compassionate eyes of the King of Glory.

"I want you to know that you were worth it to me," he said sitting next to her.   "And that my work is finished.[143] It's all over.   The battle between us is over, I have made peace.   You and I, we are reconciled.   We are not enemies anymore."

Tears came to Kamea's eyes, and he quietly sat next to her for a while.   They watched some butterflies flying from wildflower to wildflower.   In the distance, Kamea could hear the sounds of the war.   Here, she was safe.   She was rescued from that life.   She softly whispered, "Thank you."

He took her hand and, lightly squeezing it, said gently, "You are very welcome."   In a moment he rose, and they began the walk back.

It was an interesting peace.   Kamea was aware how very costly it had been for the King of Glory to reconcile her to himself ... and how amazing it was that he would offer this peace to all of those people seeking to destroy him and his Kingdom.   She felt safe and grateful.   A very quiet joy filled her heart.   It was all quite sobering.

The King of Glory interrupted her thoughts by announcing, "Tomorrow, you will go to my father's throne room and speak with him."

Terror rippled through Kamea.   "No, must I?   I will be terrified!"

"Kamea, you don't need to be afraid.   You are forgiven ... You will not be condemned or accused[144] by him.   You will not be rejected ... you will be received as a daughter."

Kamea looked at him, a troubled expression on her face. She knew she should believe the King of Glory, but it was just so hard.

"Must I?"

"Yes, of course," he said with a small grin. They continued on their way, and Kamea found her thoughts quieting down as they began to talk of the beauty they observed. Before long, Kamea was again able to wholeheartedly enjoy the little delights along the path.

CHAPTER X

The Counselor and Adelaide entered Kamea's room early in the morning. She was sleeping so soundly she did not hear them come in.

"Come, Kamea, it is time for you to get dressed! This is an important day." The Counselor said.

Kamea turned over in her bed, wondering what he was talking about. Her eyes stung in the bright light, and she did not feel ready to welcome the day. Then she remembered what she was to do today and she sat up, frantic.

"Oh no, I have to go see the Almighty One. Oh, Counselor, do I have to go today? Couldn't it be done another time? I'm sure he's very busy and doesn't need to take time out to speak to someone like me…"

The Counselor turned around and looked at Kamea with a gentle smile on his face and a sparkle in his eye. "And what exactly is 'someone like you?'"

Kamea thought silently to herself, "Someone disgraceful and unclean and worthless … someone who doesn't matter

... someone ... small." Realizing her face betrayed her thoughts, she tried to brighten her expression.

"Kamea, do you know who you are?"

Kamea looked up at him, confused by such a question. She felt ashamed. She thought she *should* know the answer, but she wasn't sure she did. Adelaide left a tray and slipped out the door.

"Do you know what your name means?"

Kamea was startled by this change of topic. "Uh…"

"You were given a new name … do you know what it means?" His voice was calm and patient.

"No, I guess I don't. I – I didn't know it *meant* anything."

He sat down next to Kamea and began to gently explain, "Your parents named you Moncha. Moncha means 'alone.'"

Kamea felt a new thorn pierce deep in her heart.

"Alone," she said as she stared at her empty hands in her lap. She felt the weight of it. She had always been alone. Always…until the day the King of Glory came. Her eyes were growing glassy with tears.

"But, Kamea, your new name, the name by which the King of Glory has always called you," he paused, his voice soothing and soft. He placed his hand gently on hers and said, almost in a whisper, "Kamea means 'precious one.'"[145]

"It does?" she said with amazement. She played with this idea in her mind. What a bright and happy thought. Precious. It seemed to glow in her heart, in a place that often ached.

"Precious," she said aloud. As soon as she said it she felt self-conscious.

"Yes, Kamea – not 'alone' – 'precious.'"

She turned and looked up at him.

"Precious." And one tear slipped silently down the side of her face and dropped into her hands in her lap.

"Precious," she whispered to herself. Inside her chest, there was a pleasant warmth ... like she could feel love coming in and filling up the empty caverns of her heart. Precious.

After a moment, the Counselor took a deep breath.

"Now, I want you to get ready to see the Almighty One. You will want to dress appropriately … so I have something to show you." He stood up and held out his hand to Kamea. He had a wide smile, and Kamea did not want to resist his direction.

She rose and took his hand. She already felt shaky from his morning visit. He guided her over to an ornate cabinet made of oak. The surface was covered with carvings, and it rested on a dresser near one of the windows in her room.

She was surprised that she had never been curious about it before. Kamea wondered what it could be. Whatever it was, it could not be better than the gift she had already received this morning; her new name.

"What do these carvings say?" Kamea asked as she ran her fingers over the curved lines.

"They are ancient writings; they read: '…Since you are precious and honored in my sight, and because I love you…'"[146] He pronounced each word in that same soothing, gentle tone.

She took a deep breath and asked, "Could you say it again?"

He smiled, "Of course. '…Since you are precious and honored in my sight, and because I love you.'"

Kamea felt something like doubt gnawing at the door of her mind, but she did not let it enter this time. She breathed in deeply and smiled as wide as she had ever dared to smile in all her life. It felt as if something had been released deep inside her, like something somewhere had been freed.

"So, if we look in this cabinet, we will see your crowns."

"My crowns?!"

"Well, princesses have crowns, don't they?" he said with a smile on his face and delight in his tone.

"Well, I, uh…"

"It would not be right to go to the throne room without the proper attire."

He opened the doors and inside were several glittering tiaras. Kamea had never seen anything like them in all her life. She really hadn't even imagined things as fantastic and extravagant as these crowns now facing her. They twinkled with gemstones and precious metals. They appeared to have been crafted with care, each one with the most intricate detail. One of the crowns was covered with white diamonds, and it was so bright that it immediately caught her eye. She reached out to touch it with the tip of her fingers and...

"That one is the crown of righteousness."[147]

Kamea drew her hand back, startled. She had forgotten herself when she saw how beautiful they were.

"Don't be shy; they are yours. They are gifts from the King."

As she looked at each of them in turn, she saw one near the back on the bottom shelf. It was golden with green gems in it. It seemed familiar and particularly precious to her because it reminded her of her grandmother's wedding necklace. She reached toward it and then quickly pulled her hands back and clasped them under her chin. The thought of her grandma brought both sweetness and sadness to her heart.

"That one," he paused, seeming to sense Kamea's feelings, "that one seems perfect."

Kamea nodded, not able to speak at first. Emotion had tightened her throat. As she gained composure, she offered, "If I am to wear a crown, I would like to wear that one, please."

"I think that would be just right," her Counselor said. He very carefully pulled it out of the case and set it on a velvet tray on her dressing table. Then, he closed the crown cabinet softly. As he walked to the door, he turned and said, "I will leave you to get ready. Then, I will come back to bring you to the throne room." He turned the handle to the door and, just as he was about to shut it behind him, he turned back and said, "Don't be afraid, Precious One. It will all be wonderful."

Kamea turned and opened the wardrobe. She paged through each dress. They were all beautiful – too beautiful. She felt like she would feel awkward, like a pretender, in one of these dresses.

"What should I do?" she thought. "Which one should I choose?"

Then, she thought of what the Counselor had said about having the appropriate attire to go into the throne room.

"What if what I wear says more about what I think of the Almighty One than what I think of myself?" She carefully looked at each dress again. Which one would show honor to the King? Then, she saw it … she took it out of the wardrobe and looked back and forth between the dress and the crown she had selected. They shared the same design … the crown had patterns of intricately woven gold that had precious stones placed in the spaces … this dress had the same patterns, with golden thread woven into the fabric.

She smiled and laid out the dress on her bed. This was the right one. She was sure of it now. She changed quickly and then arranged the crown on her head. Her stomach grumbled and she realized that, in her haste, she had forgotten breakfast. She looked over to the table on the patio where her food was waiting for her. She sat down, and thought she needed to be sure to thank Adelaide later for the food. She poured some tea and spread her jam onto her now-favorite bread. She ate and drank her fill, and was beginning to feel nervous and impatient again when she heard a quiet knock on the door.

"Yes?"

The Counselor entered and asked "Are you ready? It is time."

As he spoke, Kamea sensed a heaviness come over her. She felt as though she had feared this meeting her entire life.

She had always been hiding, always been ashamed of herself and afraid. And, here she was … going to meet the One who, if the Counselor could be trusted, knew everything she had ever done, every word she had ever spoken. Was she ready? She searched her heart.

"I want you to know, no one feels equal to a meeting with the Almighty One…but it is a choice you make. You can decide to go, despite your fears. The truth is, he has called you. And he has made you enough, sufficient…he has enabled[148] you to be a co-heir with the King of Glory, and to approach the throne of the Almighty One with confidence – not confidence in yourself, but in what has been done for you by the King of Glory. You are welcome, dear one. The only question remaining is, 'Will you respond to his invitation?'"

Kamea listened attentively to the Counselor and felt a quiet resolve solidify within her.

"Yes. I certainly will not reject his invitation. I will go."

"Ah, Kamea, my dear one, I am so glad!" he said as he held out his hand. He took her arm in his and led her out the door.

They walked through many corridors and doorways, passages and halls. So many that Kamea lost track of them. And then, seemingly all at once, they were in a great hallway. There was a beautiful marble floor, and the walls shone with brilliant light. There were two great doors before them. Kamea wondered how they would pass through them; they were much too big for the Counselor and her to open by themselves. But then, the doors opened without even a touch; they just sprang open before them like clouds parting for the sun to shine through. The Counselor slowed his step and then stopped. He turned to face her and took her hands in his.

"Through your faith in the King of Glory, you have been given the ability to approach the throne of grace of the Almighty One with freedom and confidence, precious one. You may present your requests, receive mercy and find grace to help you.[149]

"Go now."

CHAPTER XI

Kamea took a step into the room. "One step at a time." she told herself. She took a deep breath and took another step. The only sound she could hear at first was the tapping of her slipper on the floor and her own breath coming quickly. She felt joyous excitement and something like terror at the same time.

"It will be wonderful," the Counselor had said.

"It will be wonderful," she kept repeating in her mind. She tried to trust his words.

As she emerged from the doorway, she saw that the large hall did not have a back wall. Instead it had a series of white columns. Beyond them was what appeared to be some kind of courtyard, or was it a garden? Kamea walked toward it, hearing her steps echo in the giant hall. When she got to the edge of the room, she noticed that a large curtain hung in fragments at each side of the back wall. It appeared to have been torn in two. She took another breath and then stepped onto the cool grass. All about her was fragrant and fruitful. She saw flowers and produce she had never seen before, not even in the other parts of the Kingdom of Light. She was so overwhelmed with the beauty of it that she forgot entirely why she was there. She heard a waterfall in the distance and some sweet music – was it voices? Then, all at once, she found herself in a wide open space. And there, in the middle, was the great throne.

She knelt down immediately, fear gripping her heart. How disrespectful! What must he be thinking? "Will he punish me? What will happen?" Kamea worried to herself. She felt her body begin to shake and she thought she might hyperventilate. She could see only the grass beneath her. Then, she heard the most grand and rich voice. She knew it was the Almighty One.

"Do not be afraid, my child." And she sensed the Almighty One rising from the throne and approaching her.

Kamea did not know what to do so she stayed as she was, frozen.

"Dear Kamea, I take delight [150] in you. You are favored[151] of the Lord. You have been bought back[152] by the payment of my Son. You…" She felt him lay his hand upon her shoulder, "You are my daughter."[153]

Kamea felt her heart would burst. These words … these words were the answer … they were the answer to the longing of her heart. She felt them soothe the deep hurt within her. She did not know how to respond. She began to weep.

"Oh, Kamea, I draw close the brokenhearted and I save those who are crushed in spirit.[154] I heal the wounded, dear one. I am so glad you have come."

Kamea listened intently, but still could not raise her head or move from her place. She just cried and cried. It felt as if she was crying out all the years of fears and doubts … All the years of rejection and hurt … She was crying out the confusion, the loneliness and the pain. It was all given voice in her tears. She felt a great groan form within her.

"You can let it out, now, little one. You can let it go."

She cried out. She released all of her emotion. She cried out for her Lord to save her. It was messy and loud. She would have tried to refrain but she had just enough hope that this One, this One was both able and willing to help her. So, she opened up and let it all out. Her body shook with the force of it. But she let it out. She cried, she wailed and she sobbed.

And the Holy, Almighty One did not tell her to stop. He did not leave her alone. He simply kept his hand on her shoulder[155] and listened. Then, he spoke softly.

"I am here. I am close to all those who call on me.[156] If you draw near to me, I will draw near to you,[157] Precious Kamea. Long before it was your desire to come to me, it was my desire to have you come. I have loved you with an everlasting love[158] – I have drawn you to me."[159]

Kamea sensed the Almighty One's great patience. She heard his gentle words and sensed his compassion in them. He was not afraid of her emotion. He was not frustrated with her. He was completely in control and at peace. Kamea let the tears continue to flow, but she could feel the intensity waning. And then, she was being lifted up.

"Come with me, Holy and Dearly Loved."[160]

Kamea's face was now buried in the great shoulder of the Almighty One. She did not dare look at him, but she was now in his arms. She felt a safety she had never known. In this great refuge, she could not be harmed. She felt like a young bird when it is sheltered under the wings of its powerful mother.[161] She leaned into the Almighty One. She felt quieted[162] in the midst of his protection.

"Kamea, before I created the world, I chose you,"[163] he said to her. Kamea marveled at these words. She had wanted all her life for someone to choose her. Usually she would reason why this could not be so … but this time the words came, and there was faith in her heart for them to take root. She believed this powerful and loving Almighty One. She believed he had created the world. She purposed in her heart to believe all that he spoke to her.

"He chose me," her heart mused.

"I chose YOU, to be holy and blameless in my sight."

59

The Almighty One continued, "I always wanted you to be pure and without blemish. I did not want anything to separate us, so that we could always be as we are now. Even as evil entered the world, I did not let that part us forever. I had a plan that would bring reconciliation ... a plan that cost my dear and only son's suffering and death."

As he paused, Kamea thought of the King of Glory's great compassion and generosity.

"That work is done. It is finished. You did not do it, and you cannot undo it. It is finished. You have accepted his gift; you have made him your Lord. There is peace between you and me."[164]

Kamea thought of what he was saying. She remembered how the King of Glory had explained to her that there was no longer a chasm between them. How he had paid the price to bring her near. It was all beginning to take root within her. She was beginning to understand that which seemed unfathomable just a few days before.

All of this; the deliverance, the rescue, being a daughter, being a friend ... it did not depend on anything she had done, or even would do in the future. [165] It was all independent of her, really, even though it was done in her favor. The Almighty One had chosen her. He had saved her, not because of anything she had done, but according to his own purpose and grace.

"Dear Kamea, this grace was given you before the beginning of time, and now it has been revealed to you."

Kamea just rested in the Almighty One's arms. She let these words sing in her heart. Chosen. Holy. Blameless. Reconciled. Peace. Grace. She felt a deep happiness welling up inside of her. She felt a smile come to her lips.

"Be still, dear Kamea, Be still and know that I am the Lord.[166] Be still."

Kamea rested there. After a while, questions began to fill her heart. She did not dare speak, and yet they seemed to burn and fester within her. Finally, she could not resist any longer.

"Almighty One, sir?" she blurted out.

"Yes, Precious One?" he answered patiently.

"You chose me before the creation of the world?"

"Yes. You were my idea. Everything that has been made has been made by me. I created your inmost being ... I knit you together in your mother's womb. Your frame was not hidden from me when you were woven together in that secret place. All the days of your life were known to me before you were even born."[167]

"You know every word before I even speak it?"[168]

"Yes, Dear One."

Kamea could sense the pleasure in the Almighty One's voice, "You have been learning from the Counselor."

"I have tried," she said, still not wanting to move. Her mind was active and trying to grasp that this Almighty One had known her, and even created her. She had never thought of that.

"Did I turn out the way you wanted me to? Are you disappointed?"

Kamea braced herself for his answer, "Kamea, I love you. I delight in you. I made you on purpose. I wanted you."

Kamea's heart jumped.

"He wanted me?" she thought to herself.

He continued, "I am not like people that I should get disappointed. Sin grieves me, and yet I still see you for who you are becoming. I know those who are mine.[169] I know you better than you know yourself."[170]

Kamea pondered this in her mind. How could he know her better than she knew herself ... and yet, if he had known her since she was a child...and known her every step, her every word, her every thought ... perhaps he did know her better than she knew her own self. And he had not just been observing her ... he had made her.

He continued, "I know all things. I know all that has happened ... and all that will happen in the future. It is all laid out before me."

He paused and whispered right into her ear as he held her close, "I will never, ever reject you or abandon you."

Those words spoke deeply to Kamea, as if he knew the deepest question of her heart. She could not respond; she was crying again.

"Even if your mother and father abandon you, I will take care of you and hold you close."[171]

Kamea cried out, "They did abandon me! They did desert me! They left me! They left me with people who hated me! Everyone in my life has always rejected me, hated me … even my grandma … she left me, she died. I needed her, and she died! I was all alone!"

"You are not alone. I am with you.[172] I have always been with you, but in the past you did not know me. I will never leave you. I will never forsake you. I am with you. I will take care of you. I have brought you here. You will only be alone if you choose to abandon me."

Kamea felt these words soothing the hurt and anger … but the sting was not completely gone. There was still some bitterness brewing deep in her heart.

"Kamea, I rejoice that you have joined us here in the Kingdom of Light. It has been my will that you would be here, and that you would know me[173] as I have known you."

Kamea's heart was quieted by his words.

"It has pleased me greatly to adopt you as my daughter. I bless you now, to be filled with the knowledge of my will through all wisdom and understanding, that you might do good deeds and grow in the knowledge of the King."[174]

He then lifted her off his lap and set her on the floor. She did not lift her eyes to look at him. She still did not dare.

"Come back often to meet with me."[175]

Kamea felt a mixture of longing to remain in his safe arms and soft words, but also fear for his awesome power.

"Yes sir," was her simple reply. She turned around and walked slowly back toward the doors, wondering how she could possibly open them herself. She needn't have worried, for they opened again before her, just as they had earlier. When she emerged, the Counselor was waiting for her.

"How was your meeting?" he asked.

"Wonderful," Kamea said wistfully. "Wonderful," she repeated softly to herself.

CHAPTER XII

Kamea began to relax and enjoy the kingdom after her visit with the Almighty One. She met daily with her Counselor and had her lessons during her hearty breakfasts which were always delivered with a warm smile from Adelaide. She would sometimes go for walks with Saoirse or Adelaide and she started making new friends in the Kingdom of Light. She let herself begin to hope that maybe all this was not too good to be true.

One day, during the morning lesson, the Counselor walked over to the covered mirror in Kamea's room.

"Kamea, I believe it is time that you started using this mirror."

"Really? Have I been here long enough now?"

"I think you are ready, and it is important that you see yourself clearly. How you perceive yourself affects what you believe, and how you behave. You need to see yourself the way the Almighty One sees you, through the lens of his Son, the One and Only."

He paused, looking at the mirror and fingering the cloth that hid the glass underneath. Then he became aware of himself and said,

"I will give you some time; this is a very personal lesson. I will see you after dinner."

"Thank you Counselor," Kamea said as he walked out the door. She walked up to the large, free standing mirror. She had often gazed at it during the last few weeks and wondered what it was like. Why would it need to be covered? What would it show her? She reached up to touch the white, silken cloth. Her hand was just about to touch it when the thoughts came to mind,

"Are you really ready to see yourself? What if you haven't changed at all? Could you take it? Could you really survive the disappointment of it? Once you have looked, you can not go back. You cannot forget what you have seen."

Kamea struggled with her thoughts. She wanted to do what the Counselor directed her to do, but she was afraid. The idea, "Maybe you should check in your own mirror first," came to mind.

"Yes," she thought, "then I will know if I'm ready to look in the big mirror. She sat down and slid out her own shadowy mirror; she had not looked in it for a couple of weeks, and was feeling quite hopeful. She was almost sure she would see a big difference in herself. When she pulled out the mirror, though, she saw what she had always seen. She was soiled and dirty. Her face was shameful and wicked. Her eyes were dull and she was worthless. How could anyone ever love that image?

Kamea's heart sank and she slid from the edge of her bed onto the floor and wept. She cried and cried and almost missed dinner. At her meal she did not eat much. She looked at all the free and happy people and wondered how they could stand to be around her. She was wicked, worthless and shameful. She had always brought evil wherever she went. She had always been to blame. She began to wonder if they all just pretended to like her, because they were so nice. Maybe they just pitied her. Or maybe, maybe they were not nice at all and they secretly made fun of her. Maybe she was just here to be a big joke for them all.

That night, after dinner, the Counselor came in as he said he would. Adelaide followed him and busied herself with tidying up. He glanced over to the covered mirror and then to Kamea, who was already in bed.

"I am so tired tonight, Counselor, I'd like to go to sleep," she said quietly.

"Dear Kamea, would you like to talk about anything?"

"No. I don't think so," Kamea said pulling her covers close to her and shutting her eyes tightly against the tears. She did not want to tell the Counselor what she had been thinking; how she doubted his goodness and the kindness of the others in the Kingdom of Light. She wanted him to go away.

His voice broke into her thoughts.

"Well, perhaps you will let me tell you a bedtime story."

Kamea really did not want him to stay, but it seemed he was not going to take no for an answer; he was already pulling up a chair next to her bed and taking a seat.

With her face still pressed into the pillow she said, "Okay."

"One time, in a garden not so far from here, a mother duck laid several eggs in a nest. One sunny afternoon, while she was distracted by some mischievous chipmunks, one of her eggs wiggled out and rolled away from her nest. It came to rest in a well-worn path and sat there, vulnerable and alone. Soon, a good-natured boy passed by and, noticing the wayward egg, decided he would put it back where it belonged. He looked around to determine where the egg had rolled from. He soon located a nest in the sand close to the nearby pond and placed the egg snugly next to six companions. He walked away, feeling good about his heroic deed and imagining the parents of the egg filled with joy and relief upon noticing its return. In fact, it would have been a lovely gesture if it were not for the unfortunate fact that he had not put the duck egg back in its mother's nest, but had mistakenly put it into an unknowing turtle's nest."

At this, Kamea's curiosity was piqued and she began to listen more intently.

"When all the eggs hatched a few days later, and the newborn creatures emerged from their shells, there were six slimy green ones and only one fuzzy yellow one. The little fuzzy duck looked around and saw the mama turtle and the six little green turtles and assumed he was just like them. He followed the mama's example and began to swim like the turtles did, and eat what they ate. After just a short time, though, the mama turtle and six little turtles recognized the fuzzy yellow guy did not belong. They tried to convince him to fly away and find the other ducks. Kamea, do you think he left the turtles to fly with the ducks?"

"Why, of course," Kamea said. "He's a duck. They all fly."

"Well, he never did."

Kamea was annoyed at his answer.

"Well, why not?" she asked, pulling her face out of the pillow and turning toward her Counselor.

"Because no one could ever convince him he was a duck."

Kamea's nose wrinkled up and she furrowed her brow. The Counselor continued,

"He thought they were all wrong. He was sure he knew who he really was, and no one could persuade him to the contrary." The Counselor sighed, "He swam like a turtle his whole life, denying his destiny as a duck." He paused and looked into Kamea's concerned eyes, "He never flew."

"Well, that is a sad story," Kamea said, irritated and confused.

"Yes, it is, Kamea. It really is." And the Counselor got up and walked towards the door. "I hope you sleep well tonight."

"Thank you," Kamea said, a bit bewildered.

"And Kamea?"

"Yes, Counselor?"

"I hope you dream about flying."

With that, he was gone. Adelaide appeared and asked, "Is there anything I can get you, Kamea? You don't seem yourself."

"No, no, I'm fine, thanks Addie."

"All right then, goodnight."

And with that the door was closing behind her.

Kamea turned over and pondered these things in her heart. Why did the Counselor tell her that story? Did he think she was like that duck? Did he think *she* believed she was one thing, when really she was something else?

Kamea turned these thoughts over and over in her mind. If she wasn't what she grew up thinking she was, if she really wasn't dirty and worthless, would she recognize the truth when she heard it? Would she trust those who told her she wasn't what she had always thought she was? Or would she be stubborn, like that duck?

Kamea went to sleep pondering it all and was soon dreaming...dreaming of flying.

CHAPTER XIII

The next morning, Kamea awoke with new confidence. She was up and dressed when the Counselor came in, and she invited him to sit at the breakfast table.

"Counselor?" Kamea started as she poured out the tea.

"Yes, Kamea?"

"Would today be a good day to visit the Almighty One? Do you know if he is too busy?"

The Counselor sat back in his chair and looked up smiling at Kamea, who was still holding the teapot above him. He said, "I know that he is not too busy to see you." Kamea nodded and sat the teapot down, and they continued their conversation. After breakfast, Kamea took time to prepare herself to go see the king. She chose another crown and gown, and was ready and waiting when the Counselor came for her.

The Counselor escorted Kamea down to the throne room. This time, Kamea did not hesitate. She ran through the doors, her slippers sliding on the marble, and continued running to find the Almighty One. When she came into his presence, she again fell to her knees. She could not bring herself to look upon him, though she could sense that he was glorious.

He took her in his arms and began speaking to her, "I am so pleased you came to meet with me today." His words were warm, rich, vibrant and penetrating. Kamea felt her soul warmed by his presence.

He continued, "Darling one, you were my idea. I chose you before the creation of the world to be holy and dearly loved[176]… I formed you before you were born.[177] I have known every word before you spoke it.[178] I chose you, I designed you and I love you. I wanted you! You are more precious to me than you are to anyone else in the world, and I love you. Your own parents could not love you more."[179]

"Your own parents could not love you more…" Kamea repeated in her own mind. She paused to think of her parents' abandonment and her relatives' neglect; there really wasn't any comparison.

Then she thought of her grandmother. Kamea's grandmother had, for a few years, lived with her aunt and uncle, too. She had died when Kamea was still quite young. Kamea's grandmother had loved her more than anyone else ever had – until she met the One and Only. The memories flowed full of color into Kamea's mind. She had been about ten years old…

"Moncha, little one, come for a walk with me," Granny said.

Moncha looked up at her aunt and uncle, waiting for them to forbid it, but they both ignored the invitation so Moncha ran out the door holding Granny's hand. As they walked, Granny pointed out the few specks of beauty in the shadowy, bleak world. Moncha felt the kindness radiate from her Granny's face. They sat down by the spring on a fallen log so Granny could rest.

"Moncha, I am old and I will not live much longer." Moncha tightened her grip on her Granny's hand.

"Oh, don't worry child, I'm not going on today! No, but it won't be too long in coming. I wanted to tell you that when I die, I want you

to have this." Granny took the gold necklace with the green stones out of her pocket and showed it to Moncha. Moncha marveled at it.

"It's so beautiful!" Moncha said. "I have never seen this before!"

"No, I know. I have kept it secret so that it can be yours. If your aunt and uncle knew about it, well, they would give it to Lamara, I'm sure of it. But I, I want you to have it, Moncha. You see, your grandfather gave it to me as my wedding present, and I wore it to our wedding. He was a rare man. He was good to me. I hope that you can find a man like that, and that you will wear this necklace at your wedding."

Kamea remembered that conversation and how she had cried for days when her precious Granny had died several months later. The love of her grandma had, for a time, created a warm buffer between her and the harsh realities of her aunt and uncle's hatred.

"My Granny loved me," Kamea said out loud as she emerged from her memories.

"Yes, I know," responded the deep, gentle voice.

"But then she died."

"Yes."

"She died and left me all alone."

"And that made you angry."

Kamea felt the anger and confusion flood her heart, "Yes. Yes, it did." She felt an almost physical pain in her chest. It was all so clear in this moment. "It was all too much, the pain was overwhelming. The one person who cared, the only one who ever loved me ... so I took the necklace and I ran away." Kamea's voice betrayed her bitterness and her eyes became cold.

"It was mine, I didn't steal it."

"What did you do with it?"

Kamea's brow furrowed. She did not like this memory. "You know what I did."

She took a deep breath and said,

"I sold it."

"Why do you think you feel so bad about doing that, if it was yours anyway?"

Kamea was shocked at first that he seemed to know her so well, but then the Counselor had told her that he knew everything she ever did, said or even thought throughout her whole life. As she pondered his question, she realized she didn't know exactly why she felt so bad; she had never wanted to turn around and look at it straight on. She had been running away from that ache for years... but maybe now, here, she could stop and look at it.

"I don't know," she said, the anger leaving now and a strange peace coming over her.

"I can reveal it to you, if you want to know," the Almighty One said softly.

"Yes. Please do," Kamea whispered, her mouth suddenly dry.

"You feel bad because you know that you sold the necklace instead of waiting for your wedding like your grandma wanted you to do. You felt angry at her for leaving you, even though she didn't want to leave you. And so, in your bitterness you punished her by selling her necklace. You sold her dream for you. It was your way of taking revenge. But," the King pulled Kamea closer to him and said softly and clearly, "revenge never makes people feel better."[180]

"You are right," Kamea said, tears forming in her eyes, "I see it clearly now."

She started laughing at herself.

"I was so foolish. I sold it for so little and soon didn't have enough money to live on." She said laughing harder, "Some revenge!"

"Revenge will always leave you empty, little one."

Kamea got quiet. "I'm sorry I did it; my Granny had always been so kind to me. How could I have gotten so angry at the one person who was good to me?"

"Kamea, anger often separates people from those who love them. Your anger[181] separated you from me."

72

"From you?"

"Yes, you have been angry at me, haven't you?"

Kamea wanted to deny it, but then she realized it was true. She felt very quiet and small.

"Yes. Yes, I have been angry at you, for, well, for a long time really. I've been angry at you for letting my parents leave me and...and for taking my Granny. You... you..."

"You thought I could have stopped it, didn't you?"

"Couldn't you have?" Kamea asked crying and turning into his shoulder.

"Not everything is simple in this life. It is not possible for you to understand everything. What you need to decide is if you can trust that I love you, even though I have allowed you to go through difficult things in your life."[182]

He paused, and Kamea did not say anything. He started again.

"Your grandmother loved you very much. She gave you all she had. She wanted only good things in life for you. But, however much she loved you, I love you more."

Could it be true that this Almighty One could love her more that her Granny had loved her? She wanted desperately to believe it ... it was like her soul thirsted[183] for nothing more. She could feel it as a pain deep within her. But how could that be true?

She turned away from the Almighty One and slid her hand slowly down her side until she could feel the shape of her mirror inside her skirt pocket. She slipped it out just a bit and tried to catch a glimpse of herself ... she could make out the same old image: Dirty, worthless, unlovable. Nothing had changed. She sighed.

"When will you give up your old mirror and use the one I have offered you, little one?"

Kamea was embarrassed and slid the mirror quickly back into her pocket. She tried to think of a clever and fine-sounding excuse; a skill she had fine-tuned over the course of her life, but she found that, in the Almighty One's presence, she was unable to do so.

He rose. Kamea was afraid she had angered him, but then he extended his hand.

"Will you walk with me today?"

Kamea was relieved that she didn't have to answer his hard question about the mirror. She wanted to believe him so badly, and even though it seemed so unlikely that he could love her in the way he described ... he had not yet lied to her. She decided to trust him.

She took his hand, and they walked through the lovely garden in the cool of the day. Her tumultuous emotions began to calm down and she was able to enjoy the walk and even laugh. She left his presence feeling emotionally tired, but content.

CHAPTER XIV

Every morning after that, Kamea paused in front of the great mirror in her room as she got ready for her lesson with the Counselor. She longed to know what she would see in it. Was she really lovely and clean and radiant, as the Counselor said she was and like all the others in this Kingdom; or was she still, as she often feared, the same as ever? Could she really change?

Mara had changed. She had been transformed into Saoirse. As Kamea had talked with her, she had sensed a liberty within Saoirse. She was free from hatred and bitterness. She was so tender and compassionate now instead of hard and hateful. She smiled and laughed easily. It was as if Saoirse was the best version of Mara. The same person, and yet freed from the shadows of the Dominion of Darkness.

There was so much reason to believe the Counselor, the King of Glory and the Almighty One, and yet doubt was always with her. She found her hand rubbing over the mirror in her pocket unconsciously during the day. It was a constant reminder of her stinging past.

"If only there was a way to be free of it all," she mused. "If only I could be new, like all of these people."

One morning the Counselor came in at lesson time and brought a wooden bucket with him. Kamea was curious and noticed it was empty.

"What's that for?" she asked with a smile in her eyes.

"Oh, Kamea, today is a special day for you! You have learned and grown so much since you've been here, and it is time for you to join the others in serving in the Kingdom."

Kamea thought of the artists, dancers and gardeners, and her heart delighted.

"What will I do? Will I paint ... or sing?! Or will I learn to dance or to trim bushes into those delightful shapes?!"

The Counselor took the bucket and held it out to her with a smile.

"To start, you will go to the spring every morning and bring fresh water back to the castle for the King of Glory."

"What?!" she said, not hiding her horror. "What do you mean?"

"That is the service you have been assigned. That is your way of expressing worship."

"No. No, I won't do it." She stepped back, shaking her head. Her mind was reeling. What was happening? All this time she had been here – being treated like a princess – was it all a joke? She was going to have to bring the water up, as she had ever since she could walk? She shook her head and cried,

"No!"

Then she ran past the Counselor and out the door, shouting, "No, No I won't, I can't!"

Kamea ran out of the great house. She ran to the trees, her favorite place to hide. She paced, not knowing what to do. How could they assign her such a job?

"It's all as it ever was," her thoughts accused. "Nothing has changed. They pretend to honor you, but they are like all the rest."

"Like all the rest!" Kamea wondered. "But they care about me…"

"So they treat you like a princess and then give you the same worthless job you have always had?" the accusations continued. Then, they changed tone, "Of course, that could be because that is all you are good for. They tried to be nice to you, but you really don't belong here. There is nothing else you are suited for but fetching the water. So, now, instead of doing it until you die, you can do it for all time!"

At the thought of this, doom closed in around Kamea.

"I cannot stay here! I can't! I must leave. I must leave right now!" Kamea turned to run away,

"Of course. You always run away. That is who you are," the condemning thoughts continued. She ran and ran and ran.

As Kamea ran, she felt the bitterness eating away inside of her. It was impossible to live this way; to always be good. To always obey. To believe impossible things. She had to get away. She had to get away and think. Suddenly, she craved her old life. She wanted things to be familiar again. Things had changed so quickly – too quickly.

She thought about her old life and about the things she was struggling to believe that the Almighty One had told her. That she was chosen, known, loved. That she was wanted. All of the shadows of the old life came back into her mind. She felt the old dread. She was so confused. She had been running aimlessly. She was now far from the King's mountain and it was late, and the land was growing dark. She deduced she must have left the Kingdom of Light and she realized she was unprotected and alone.

She slowed her steps as fear crept in. It felt familiar, but certainly not friendly. Every noise seemed like an attack, and her heart jumped within her. She realized now that she was exhausted. She was not certain how to even return to the Kingdom of Light, or if she'd be allowed to. She kept wandering because she did not know what else to do. It

77

began to rain, and her dress was quickly soaked through. The wind chilled her and she became desperate. The wet dress was heavy, and it was hard to keep her legs moving. Kamea cried out, "Help me!" and then, in the next step, there was nothing there to hold her up. She felt herself falling, then she hit the bottom. There was water in the pit from the rain, and it had made the miry clay bottom both mucky and slippery.[184]

Kamea was crying now.

"Is this how I am going to die? All alone in this pit? Oh, I deserve it. I do. I am nothing but ungrateful and evil. I do not matter anyway. My parents were right to abandon me. This is it. This is the end."

She turned to face the top of the pit. The rain was falling down into the pit and into her eyes.

"I am lost. I am so lost." Then, she sat down in the water. She laid her head against the side of the pit. She sat still for a long while. The word "Help" was on her lips.

She thought of the King of Glory and how he had rescued her that first day. He was her hero. The One who saves. She thought of how he had sung, rejoicing when he had rescued her.[185] She thought of her new name. Kamea. "Precious One." She thought of the fine clothes and crowns … and of the direction and encouragement of her Counselor. Was it all real? Could she have stayed? She longed to be there now. She longed to be enjoying dinner with the others.

She reached her hand upward and slid it along the wall. It was muddy and slick. There was no way to climb it, this pit was nearly twice her height. There was no way she could get out. Water continued pouring into the pit. Sitting with her hands wrapped around her knees she watched as the inches of water around her grew. She was soaked through to the skin. Shivers ran up her spine. She was helpless. There was nothing she could do. Nothing. Nothing but wait to die. If the rain continued, was it possible that the pit would fill up? If it didn't would she just starve to death? Kamea felt a worm wriggling in the dirt beneath her. Would he soon be eating her remains?

"Oh, King, I am so needy. I am so lowly and weak. You are my Help. Please come…"[186] she cried aloud from her heart. The storm was raging above her now. The rain had been joined by thunder and terrible winds. She watched it from the bottom of her pit.

"Kamea!" she suddenly heard above the sound of the rain. "Kamea!"

"Who was that?" she thought. Someone was coming.

Kamea stood up and shouted as best she could, "I'm here, I'm here." But the thunder roared just as she yelled and drowned out her voice. Her heart that had just been filled with hope was beginning to despair again. She took a deep breath and cried from deep in her heart … he must hear me … he must! "I'm here! Help me, please!"

Just then she saw the King of Glory, in all his glowing radiance at the mouth of the pit.

"You came for me?!"

"I will always come for you, Kamea." And he reached his hand deep into the pit.[187] "Always."

Kamea felt a warmth in her heart that overcame every shiver the rain and fear had caused. "Will you take my hand?"

Kamea looked at him and thought of how she had wandered away. She longed to be with him.

"Yes," she said as she clasped both hands tightly about his. He swiftly lifted her from the pit.

When she emerged, she saw that he was soaking wet and very dirty. One of his hands was bloody, and he had a cut on his forehead.

"What happened to you?" Kamea said.

"I was searching for you everywhere.[188] I climbed a cliff and some of the rocks were sharp. As I was nearing this place, I came across a frightened mountain lion and I had to get past him to get to you."

Kamea looked at his wounds, "And you kept looking for me?"

"I will always come for you, Kamea. Always."

Kamea looked at the earnestness in his eyes. She wanted to believe him. He deserved so much to be believed. As tears filled her eyes, she ripped part of her skirt and made a bandage. She wrapped up his hand with it, then started making another bandage for the cut on his forehead. "Thank you," he said.

Kamea could not continue. She was overcome with tears as she knelt there next to him in the rain. "I am not worth this! I am not worth all this pain! All this effort!"

"Yes, you are Kamea." He put his arm on her shoulder. "You are, because I have decided you are."[189]

"Won't the Almighty One be mad that you came after me?"

"No, not at all … I only do what he wills, Kamea. He is not willing that any of his Little Ones would be lost."[190] He looked her in the eye. "You have been adopted,[191] Kamea. You are part of our family. Do you think so little of us that you think we would abandon you now, after paying the price for you[192] and rescuing you from the Dominion of Darkness?"

Kamea was struck with this statement. "Think so little of them?" she wondered to herself. "Think so little of them, that they would abandon me? I thought I was putting down myself, not them. I am not worthy … but if he decides that I am worthy, then his behavior depends on his character, his decision … not on what I do."[193] Kamea was amazed and speechless.

"Come, Precious One. We must get back to the others and out of the rain." He got up and put out his hand to help her up. She had a furrowed brow as she rose and took a few steps with him.

"My King?" Kamea said.

He turned to her and smiled, "Yes?"

"Thank you."

Kamea hugged him tightly.

"Thank you so much for coming for me. Thank you so much for rescuing me. Thank you ... thank you for deciding to love me."

The King of Glory wrapped his arms around Kamea.

"You are welcome, Dear, Precious One. You are welcome."

As they walked back, a song filled Kamea's heart ... a hymn of praise. She felt she would burst from the pressure of it if she did not give it voice ... so she sang:

"I was lost in the darkness...
My hope drifting away...
I was drowned in my fears...
Then you came ... then you came ... then you came

You rescued me
Put my feet on firm rock
You rescued me
Put a new song in my heart
You rescued me
Put my feet on the rock
You rescued me
Put a new song in my heart ... in my heart

I will sing ... I will sing ... I will sing...
Praise to my King.
Praise to my King."[194]

CHAPTER XV

As they neared the castle, the light returned, the rain slowly stopped and they began to feel warmth again. Kamea had stopped singing over the last mile. Something was bothering her. The King of Glory asked her, "Kamea, what is it that has stolen your joy?"

Kamea sighed.

"What will the others think of me, now that I refused to do my job and I wandered away like that?"

The King of Glory stopped walking. He took her hand and sat down with her on a fallen log.

"Do you think no one else has ever lost their way?"

Kamea looked at him, stunned.

"They are all like you, Kamea, and it is not always easy for the citizens of the Kingdom of Light to adjust to their new lives. It takes time for each person to learn about how they have changed ... and to come to know me and my father."

He looked at her, smiling now.

"You are not the first one I have had to find in the darkness."[195]

"Really?" she said. Everyone looked so perfect; she had not imagined that any of them had ever struggled.

"Yes! There is room in our Kingdom to grow,"[196] he said, looking up at the tops of the trees, and then back at her, "And part of growing is making mistakes."

"I don't want to make any more mistakes. I have made so many in my life," Kamea said, looking down at the ground, shame filling her face.

"I know ... but you will most likely be making a few more in your life. And," he took her hand and clasped it in his own, "and I will still be here. I am able to keep you from stumbling and to enable you to come before my father and me, blameless..." He paused and squeezed her hand, "...with great joy."[197]

Kamea noticed the look in his eye and saw his love for her. She thought of her song and the joy she had experienced when she had given up resisting him and just received the love he offered ... when she had decided to believe him.

"Maybe it is better to be loved ... than to be perfect," she said, a quiet confidence filling her heart.

The King of Glory smiled back at her and rose, "Maybe it is," he said as he led her back to the castle.

The next afternoon, Kamea rose and dressed quickly. She reflected on how happy everyone had been to see her when she returned late in the night. She expected condemnation. She expected to be called stupid and ungrateful ... but none of that had happened. People had seemed genuinely glad to have her back. Saorise had come running up to her and hugged her, and Adelaide had left a snack for her in her room. As she walked back to her room, she heard a faint song of rejoicing reverberating in the halls. She wondered if it could be for her. She changed into dry clothes and slept soundly after her ordeal. She felt safe.

Kamea was nervous for one more meeting. The Counselor would be coming for her lesson soon, and she was not sure she wanted to face him. She was pacing before her bed and biting her bottom lip, unable to eat the hearty brunch Adelaide had delivered, when she heard the door handle turn. She felt her face redden and grow hot as she saw the Counselor. Before he was fully through the door, she blurted out, "I am so sorry that I wandered away."

He looked at Kamea with merciful eyes. "Kamea, I am so glad that you have come back."

"I – I hope you will still teach me. I still want to learn."

"I am always eager to share my counsel with you, if you desire to hear it."

And he gave a slight bow.

Kamea felt tears form in her eyes.

"This is extravagant kindness. I am so sorry I doubted you."

"You have turned around. You are back. And for that, I rejoice,"[198] the Counselor said. "Now then, would you like to start today's lesson?"

"Very much!" Kamea said, relief and joy filling her heart and making it light.

"Well, then you should sit down and eat your meal while I get started," he said with a smile.

Kamea blushed at his kind attention. Suddenly, she felt how very hungry she was. She sat down to bread, fruit and fish. She had a healthy appetite for the food, the company, and ... the truth. The Counselor reviewed the lessons from the beginning. He did seem to enjoy his work, and Kamea was able to understand more this time. It was a delight to be reunited with him and the others in the Kingdom of Light. Her heart glowed with joy and hope once more.

CHAPTER XVI

Kamea continued to have her daily lessons with the Counselor and nothing more was said about carrying water. One morning, as they were having their breakfast lesson the Counselor said cautiously,

"Kamea, I know that you don't like to think about your old life, but we are going to talk about it a little today." There was nothing foreboding in his tone, so Kamea kept her nerves in check until she heard where this was leading.

"Kamea, would you agree with me that you were dead in your old life?[199] In the evil things you did?"

"What ... what do you mean?"

"There was no vitality in your old life. No hope. No peace. No joy."

Kamea did not have to think long. She nodded agreement.

"Despair, self-hatred, self-centeredness, chasing after men and possessions...they are all a kind of death ... do you see what I mean? There was breath in your body, but your heart was dead. It was hard ... like a stone. You were able to be cruel to people and to rationalize that they deserved it. You were not trustworthy, and you did not trust others. You were a slave to what you felt like doing, or what you thought would satisfy the cravings and desires of your heart. You were dead. You were a slave.[200] Do you see that as you look back?"

Kamea's mind soared back to an uncomfortable memory. She thought of how she had traveled with a swindler for a few years. They would travel from village to village. The swindler, Chapman, [201] had a useless concoction he would put in old bottles he collected. He tried to pass it off as an "elixir to cure the common ills." And he was an amazing salesman. Moncha had watched him one day and was drawn in by his grand orations...

"No matter what you have, a cough, a chill, a runny nose…no matter what it is, this here will cure it, that's for sure! I have seen people who've had sores on their feet for years and this right here cured it up in a week!" Chapman proclaimed while standing on the back of his cart and holding a bottle of his "Cure–All Elixir." Moncha watched him look over the crowd, study them and then adjust his speech to fit their needs.

"Having trouble getting a good night's rest? This here will help you out. It's full of secret and potent ingredients, yes it is, and it's been known to cure about anything that ails ya, it has."

"Is it safe, really?" a woman holding a baby asked.

"Well, yes, yes of course! I've given it to my own Mum, I have. She's living still and over eighty!" he cried. With that, people were talking all amongst themselves. Moncha was watching him and had a clever thought. If she helped him sell this stuff, whatever it was, maybe he would buy her dinner. She hadn't had much to eat for days and she needed a good meal.

Moncha moved to the front of the group and put her hands on her hips, stood up straight and spoke lively and boldly, "I've used his elixir and it has cured me of the coughs! It surely has. It only took a couple bottles, and I feel the best I have in all my life."

Chapman had looked at her suspiciously for a moment, but when their eyes met, they had an understanding without saying a word.

"There you have it folks, a satisfied and healthy customer!"

After the crowd bought their fill of elixir and dispersed, Moncha found Chapman and they struck up a partnership over dinner. They developed a few different "shows" to trick people out of money in all the villages they visited. At first, it was fun. The acting and lying came easily to Moncha, and she enjoyed the attention, the good meals and better clothes; but after a while she began to feel hollow inside. She wondered about the people who were spending their last bit of money on elixir in the hopes of saving a dying loved one. She began to hate them for being so stupid as to let her trick them. She started hating herself. She even grew to despise Chapman and started picking arguments with him. Soon, they had completely fallen out of favor with one another and parted company. Moncha was left without any money or any way to make money, alone and unprotected. She dared not go back to the villages they had visited for fear the people would recognize her and demand their money back for the fake medicine. She had walked off, alone and yes, dead inside.

From that time on, Moncha had continued to use dishonesty and tricks to make her living. She hated all the stupid people who deserved to get taken advantage of. Her heart had been hard and afraid.

These thoughts were painful. Kamea tried to shake them away and swallow past the lump in her throat.

The Counselor looked Kamea in the eyes.

"Everything is changed now," he said. "Through your trust in the King of Glory, you have been made alive."[202] He spoke softly and intently, "The old is gone, the new has come.[203] You are no longer part of that 'dead' life; you have been given the life that is truly life![204]

Kamea struggled to take in these words. It was what she longed for; to be alive and full of light.[205] Could it be true? Could her dreams finally be fulfilled? Could so much death and hatred in her heart be overcome by the King's love?

The King of Glory met her by the trees. Kamea had been early again, eagerly awaiting his arrival. When she saw him, she ran right up to him and put her arms around his neck.

"What a wonderful greeting!" he said, laughing and hugging her back. "Shall we begin our walk?"

"Oh, yes!" she said. "Where shall we go today?"

"Oh, I have some ideas," he said as he took her hand and they began to walk. They talked about the beauty of the day and the brilliance of the light. They stopped and smelled some flowers. Before Kamea knew it, they were at the spring the Counselor had shown her on the tour her very first day.

Kamea's heart grew cold and angry.

"Why are we here?" she asked plainly.

"Kamea, I think we need to talk." He sat down on a bench and invited her to sit next to him. She was noticeably reluctant, but then she found her seat. A knot formed in her stomach and she couldn't stop the shaking in her legs or keep herself from biting her bottom lip.

"Kamea, work is right and good.[206] From the beginning, it has been my father's plan that his people would be occupied with useful work."[207]

Kamea sat stiffly, the words not really reaching her heart. She wanted to cry, she wanted to scream; her heart was breaking. How could the King of Glory do this to her? How could he be making her do the one thing she despised, the chore that had made her feel worthless her whole life?

"Kamea, where have you gone? Are you deep in your thoughts? Why don't you talk to me? I know that you are angry that I have asked you to get the water that we need from this spring, but I don't think you know *why* you are so angry."

Kamea heard this and was confused. Since he knew what she was thinking anyway, she thought she'd just start sharing all her ugly thoughts with him out loud.

"Why would you give me this horrible job when there are such beautiful things to do here? Some dance, some paint, some garden ... I am supposed to do something stupid and worthless like fetching the water. Anyone could do that. It is not special."

She looked him straight in his face.

"It shows what you really think of me! You hate me and you think I am nothing!"

She got up and walked a few steps away; her arms folded and tears stinging her cheeks. She wanted to run away...

"Don't run away from me; let us really talk about this. What does the job I ask you to do have to do with the value I place on you? How does it express what I think of you?"

She did not say anything; she really had nothing to say.

"Have I not told you that I chose you, I want you here, and that I love you?"

Kamea continued to listen, but did not turn around.

"Didn't I come for you, at my peril, in the Dominion of Darkness to rescue you?"

Kamea's thoughts were swirling wildly. It was true, he had done that.

"Didn't I come and rescue you from the pit when you wandered away and were lost ... when you were angry with me and hated me and accused me of all kinds of wrong-doing in your heart?"

Kamea could not argue with this. It was true. The King of Glory had shown her his love in many, many ways.

"And before you were even born, Kamea, my father had a plan to bring you here; to adopt you as his daughter. And I suffered and I died to make a way for that to happen."

Kamea's tears of anger turned to tears of shame, and she began to shake as she wept bitterly.

"Kamea, the truth is that I love you. I want you. I chose you. I delight in you. I want you to be safe. I want

89

you to know me. I have the best in mind for you. I choose the talents and tasks that I give to the world, and I chose the talents and tasks that I have given you.[208] Do you think you could trust me about this? Am I not trustworthy?"

Kamea just stood there and wept. He was right. There was no reason in the world to doubt the King of Glory's faithfulness to her. He had done her good and not harm from the very beginning. He had shown himself faithful even when she had been faithless.[209] Then, she exclaimed through her tears,

"Then, I just don't understand why!"

She sank to her knees.

"Why this? Why this stupid, ugly, simple task? Why, when I long to do something great in my worship for you? Why send me back to do the thing I have always done, as if nothing has changed?" She hid her face in her hands and just cried.

"Kamea!" the King of Glory said with authority, "You do not see rightly yet. Let me show you the truth."

Kamea was shocked and in her awe, stopped for a minute and gave the King of Glory her full attention.

"I chose this task for you because I love you. The spring has been a special place in my relationship with you. Remember, I gave you a gift on your fifth birthday at the spring."

Kamea remembered the beautiful crocus flower.

He continued.

"And the day that you fell and you were bleeding, you came to the spring to wash your wound, and then it felt better."

Kamea was more and more intrigued as she remembered.

"And Saoirse came to you as you fetched the water at the spring, do you remember?"

The pictures were clear in Kamea's mind. Yes, she remembered. Kamea could see it now.

"And I myself came to you at the spring in the Dominion of Darkness. I came because I knew you were thirsty.[210] Your whole life you have been so, so thirsty. Your whole life you have had to fetch water, and you have hated it, but I allowed this in your life to point to me ... the real water that satisfies.[211] I am the Living Water. Those who drink from me never thirst again."

"I gave you this job because I want you to be satisfied and to drink deeply of the water I give you. I want the best for you. I want abundant, overflowing life[212] for you."

Kamea was weeping, but now it was because she understood. She could see how her King had been showing himself to her again and again throughout her life. She realized that this job, which was a curse to her, had been used in her deliverance. Just as the water had relieved her body's thirst, the King of Glory had come and satisfied her deep, inner thirst to belong, to be known, to be enjoyed. He had exceeded her dreams for love in every way. He was the spring that never ran dry. He was the water that deeply satisfied.

"I see. I was blind all those years to you, but now I see the truth," she said through tears.

"And now, my precious, good and honored Kamea, now, I ask you to share this water with others. You are my water-bearer. You are called to drink deeply of this water and to offer it to others who are thirsty." And he motioned beyond the mountains. Kamea knew what he meant. She was called to go[213] out to those who were still lost in the Dominion of Darkness and share the truth, the living water, with them.

"Saoirse..." she said softly.

"Yes, Saoirse did this for you. It is a lofty calling, little one, not an ugly, worthless, stupid one. It is of the utmost importance. It is sharing life with those who are lost in darkness and death."

Kamea remained on her knees and just wept. How could she have been so wrong about him? He was offering her a lofty position, an honored place. She got up. She went to the spring and cupped her hands beneath the cold

91

water. As she rose carefully, holding as much as she could while some dripped down her arms, her tears mixed with the fresh water. She walked up to her King and she knelt and bowed before him, her hands outstretched before her.

"There was a time that you asked me for a drink," she said, "And I never gave you one. Please accept this now."

The spring was a holy sanctuary in that moment. This was Kamea's precious act of worship,[214] of surrender, of adoration to her loving King. He did not say anything, but she felt him put his hands under hers as he drank deeply from her precious cup. She had never felt such joy or honor in all of her life.

CHAPTER XVII

The next morning, Kamea awoke and put on one of the beautiful dresses from her armoire. She got ready and paused, once again, in front of the covered mirror. She reflected on the lovely time she had spent with the King of Glory at the spring the day before. Her heart glowed. And yet, as she looked at the mirror covered by the white silken cloth, she automatically slid her hand down to pat her pocket and feel the mirror that was inside. That was reality, she told herself. Not some hopeful fairy tale. "Maybe someday," was all she could come up with to encourage herself.

The Counselor came in with a lot of energy that morning. Kamea was just finishing her breakfast when he came and stood by the table.

"Today, we have an important lesson, Precious One. It is related to our previous lesson, which was that you are filled with life and light, no longer with death and darkness. Today, I want to share with you that you are a new creation, the old has gone and the new has come!"[215]

"What?" Kamea said, still foggy from the morning and not able to immediately grasp what he was saying.

93

He reached out and took her hands, pulled her up from her chair and led her over to the great mirror.

"You are a new creation, Kamea. You have been made new in the power and the love of the King. You are not as you fear you are. You are who he has made you to be! It is time for you to see the truth about yourself."

Kamea was not sure what he meant when he said "the truth" about her. She grimaced and braced herself as he pulled the cloth from the mirror. On the beautiful wooden frame it had the word "Faith" engraved on the top and, as she looked, she did not recognize what she saw. There was a woman there, a beautiful, good, pure, spotless, unblemished woman. She was radiant.[216] As Kamea studied her, she seemed faintly familiar. Kamea was stunned. She reached and touched her own face, and the woman in the reflection did the same. Kamea was speechless. That woman, could that be Kamea herself?

"This is your lesson today, Kamea. You are not who you were, you are who the Lord has said you are. He has said you are a new creation! You are pure![217] You are loved! Those who look to him are radiant; their faces are never covered with shame!"[218] He paused and watched her as she stood there, frozen before the mirror.

"This is, as I said before, a private lesson. I will give you a moment and come back later. Take your time."

And then he walked to the door and left her alone.

Kamea started crying. She could not make sense of it all. She crumpled to the floor, still staring into the mirror. What did all this mean? She slowly slid her hand down to her pocket. What would her old mirror say? Was it true? Was she finally transformed? Was she finally like the others here? Was she new like Saoirse? Like the Counselor said?

Her hand shook as she slid out the mirror. She slowly turned it and then ... she sobbed with anguish. There it was, as clear as ever, the truth! She was the same dirty, shameful and wicked creature she had always been! Kamea's heart broke.

"I can't take this anymore!" she cried. It was too much. Her hopes had been crushed for the last time. She had to get away from this place. It was going to destroy her.

She stood up and ran for the door, slipping her mirror back into her pocket. Then she turned back. She opened the beautiful case of crowns and grabbed the green and gold one. Then she turned back and ran down the corridor and down the steps. She found the door and as she broke through to the outside, the Counselor caught her hand.

"Kamea!" he said, "Kamea stop! Don't run away!"

"I have to leave!" she said, pulling away from his grasp. "I don't belong here!"

"Yes you do! You belong only here!"[219] Kamea pulled away and was running as she faintly heard him call behind her,

"Kamea, nothing can separate you from the Love of the King, nothing…"

Kamea ran and ran. She ripped her gown as she tore through branches, her skirt was muddied from the damp ground, but she did not care. Her hair became tangled with leaves and twigs; her face was full of her tears. She ran on and on as fast as she could, trying to find the way back home.

Finally, she stood at the path leading back to the Dominion of Darkness. Her heart ached in her chest. Part of her did not want to leave. She remembered the cold of the night when she had fallen into the pit. In her mind she could still see the light of the King of Glory's face as he had looked down at her, and she felt the hate well up inside her. She hated him for being so good. She hated him for the confusion. She had been fine just as she was. Why had he come for her?

It was all a lie. She would never change. It was impossible. The dread within her had been right. She began running down the path to the Dominion of Darkness,

95

tears streaming down her face. She held her skirts high as she ran and ran.

How could he have lied to her? How could he have given her hope, just to be defeated!? She had never dared to hope before, and now she saw she was right all along. It was foolish to hope for change ... to hope to be loved. Hope was a lie.[220]

All that was before her was darkness. She ran to it. She wanted it to hide her. She was sick of walking in the light,[221] of having her fears laid bare to the Counselor. She did not want to be known. She wanted to evaporate. She wanted to be covered in darkness.

It was all too hard. It was impossible. Why had she believed him? Why had she tried?

The King of Glory's loving face came into her mind, his hand extended as an invitation to join him on his horse.

"Will you trust me?"

She ran harder, trying to get away from the memory, and she fell.

She was in the mud.

She lay there, her body hurt and her heart broken, and she cried. Then, she noticed the tiara she had stolen had fallen out of her pocket and was lying in the mud. The golden glow and the green stones reminded her of her grandma's necklace. Her Granny's dream for her haunted her. Her wedding, hah! No one would ever love her the way her grandma had described. Maybe that had just been the meaningless ranting of a crazy old woman. She sat up and turned away from it. She pulled out the mirror from her pocket.

It showed her the truth. She was a liar and a thief. She was not like the others in the Kingdom of Light. She did not belong there. She saw the lewdness, the malice in her eyes. Lines of hate surrounded them and she could see the shame that always had haunted her.

No, things didn't ever change for Moncha. She was as she had always been: wicked and alone.

Her tears stopped as she resigned herself to this truth. It draped over her like a heavy cloak. She had forgotten the weight of it over the past weeks. It was familiar, but not comfortable. She leaned over, picked up the crown and put it in her pocket.

"It should get me enough to get started," she thought.

She put the mirror in the other pocket. At least she still had the mirror. At least she hadn't lost that in this wild adventure.

She continued down the path, walking now. Her feet were heavy and the land was dark. She wondered where she should go. Would Locke take her back? Should she go to a place where she was unknown? An old, familiar thirst grew within her. She decided to stop in the nearest village and try to sell the crown. She needed to forget about the Kingdom of Light as soon as possible.

CHAPTER XVIII

As Moncha walked on, she grew so tired she had to rest for the night. She found a place to lie down in the middle of some bramble bushes, and from the smell of it many animal families had lived there before. In the morning, the bleak light reached her as she awoke. She sat up, not remembering where she was. The morning dew had left her damp and chilled. She looked at what had been a white dress. It was soiled and ripped. She smiled sarcastically, "That's more like it." She grabbed a ripped place and then ripped the dress some more. "Yeah, why live a lie?"

She began walking again, and her stomach rumbled. The memories of mornings in the King's house and the wonderful breakfasts and warm smiles Adelaide would bring came to mind. She had enjoyed fullness in the house of the King, but now she was empty. As she walked, she realized how she had enjoyed not only the food, but the company of the Counselor, and of the other members of the household. She began to long for Saorise, Adelaide, Rawiya and the others, and an ache filled her heart. Moncha steeled herself and pushed away the sadness and longing with anger.

"Why did you do this to me? If I had never … then I wouldn't…" She stopped, a tear escaping. "How could you be so cruel?" She shook it off and kept walking. "I wonder where I am," she thought.

She kept walking all day and, as the modest light ebbed away, she came upon a home. She was ravenous with hunger. She waited until all the lights were out in the dwelling, then made her way to the outer building. The hay was dry and the animals made it warm. She found some discarded pottage and peas left for the pigs and began eating voraciously.

Her mind wandered to the great feasts the King had every night, celebrating the rescue of his precious ones. She pushed the uncomfortable memory away. She ate what she could swallow without gagging and then she lay down with an uncomfortable fullness. The food did not sit well. She hoped she would be able to sleep, but her stomach ached. The pain grew and kept her awake.

As she lay there in the dark, alone, she tried to think of a plan. What should she do next? Perhaps she could use the money from selling the crown and go to the tavern. At one time, she had been good at gambling. Perhaps she could multiply the money and be able to buy a deserted house and a little land, where she could have a garden, maybe a chicken or two and a pig. Perhaps she could brew ale for money, as other poor women did, and just live alone. She did not want to be hurt, or to hurt anybody else any more. She just wanted to escape to the shadows.

The pain in her stomach finally dissipated, and she slept. She awoke to the crowing of the cock the next day. She felt like she had barely slept, but she quickly stole away before anyone discovered her. She walked in the woods parallel to the path now; in her younger years, she had learned that women traveling alone had to be on their guard. She felt vulnerable and lonely. Her stomach ached. Her heart ached.

"I just have to make it to the next village," she kept telling herself.

By nightfall, she had had arrived at a village. She knelt by a brook and washed her face and hands, trying to look normal. She walked into the village, adopting a strut she used to use, and looked for the best place to try to sell the crown. She touched it in her pocket. For the first time since she took it, guilt troubled her heart.

"No, he deserves it for what he's done to me!" she told herself. Then she reasoned, "He probably won't even know that it is gone, he is so rich. And now that I am..." she paused. "Now that I am gone... he won't need it."

She went to the back door of a merchant's house. She knocked, and a man concealed by shadows answered the door.

"What do you want?" he barked. He looked at her with suspicion.

Moncha remembered her previous life and adopted an aggressive tone.

"I want to sell something of great value for a fair price."

"Oh really woman? What do you have that you think is of such great value?"

He smirked looking at her ripped dress and filthy appearance.

Moncha tried to appear confident even as her heart raced within her and fear danced about her nerves.

"This!" she said as she pulled out the tiara.

"What?!" he exclaimed. "Where did you get that?" He looked at her with wonder and mistrust.

"Does it matter? How much?" Moncha said boldly, trying to conceal the quavering in her voice.

"I'll give you my goat, Gyles."

"No. No livestock. I want something I can spend *tonight*," she said, hoping he would offer something else.

He waited, looking intently at her. Moncha tried to appear resolute. After what seemed like hours, he turned and went into the house. He came back with a little leather pouch.

"I will give you this."

Moncha took the pouch and looked inside.

"Is that all?" she said, her heart sinking.

He smiled viciously at her, "You go and try to find someone else to take that off your hands. That there's dangerous. Someone has to know how to sell something like that without attracting too much attention. No, that's all. That's all I'll give you."

Moncha took the pouch from him. Despair and hatred battled in her heart as she handed him the crown and walked away. What now? She looked up and saw a tavern down the way. She decided to go back to the brook and to compose herself before she went in to gamble the money. She planned to take this meager amount and try to make the small fortune she needed. She tried to hope, but she knew her chances of success were small.

CHAPTER XIX

Moncha took her small bag of money and followed the crooked path down to a brook. Her legs were weak under her, and she was afraid they would give way. She got on her knees and took a long drink of water. Then she sat down against a tree. Was this the life she had missed?[222] She slid her hand down to her pocket and felt the money pouch inside. She was about to get up and go to the tavern when she saw a small silhouette coming down to the brook. It was a little girl. Moncha sat very still and watched. The girl was crying and carrying a heavy wooden bucket. She walked over until she was almost within Moncha's reach, but did not notice her because of her tears.

She leaned down and filled her bucket.

Moncha's heart went out to her. She knew the heaviness this child bore.

As she pulled the bucket out of the water, the child could barely move it because of its weight.

Moncha could not bear it. She got up and grabbed the bucket to help, surprising the little one.

"Oh!" she cried as she jumped back.

"I'm sorry," Moncha said

"Who are you?" the girl asked, still crying. As she backed away, a bit of light shone on her face and Moncha could see a bruise.

"What happened to you?" Moncha asked her heart full of concern and compassion.

"Don't look," the girl said in shame. "They will get mad if you see. That is why they sent me here so late. They didn't want anyone to see. Oh, they will beat me if they find out you saw me ... please don't tell!"

Moncha looked at the child in pity.

"Why did they hit you, child?"

"They think I stole some money, but I didn't. I just lost it. I walked the cow to Alice's house, and they gave me the money."

The girl was sobbing now, and Moncha could barely make out what she was saying, "But I lost it. I don't know how I did and I looked and looked and looked. But, they don't believe me. They ... they hate me. They hit me."

Moncha looked at her with pity. She knew the pain in the girl's heart. She wished she could do something to make her feel better.

"Why do they hate you?"

"Because I am so wicked," the girl said.

"Wicked? You are just a child. You are not old enough to be so wicked," Moncha said softly. She wanted so desperately to encourage this young girl, to help her. She searched her mind for something to say and drew from a lesson the Counselor had taught her.

"You know, no one is good on their own,[223] no one except the One and Only, but we were all made on purpose.[224] We were made by a loving King. I see a spark of his beauty in you! He loves you very much."[225]

The girl looked up at her, "How come you are so nice to me?" she said. Moncha was taken aback. She didn't know how to respond. She had never once thought she was nice.

"I — I…"

Then, it came to her. "Someone was very nice to me recently."

Then, she knew what she was going to do. She took the pouch out of her pocket. "Do you think they would believe this was enough for a cow?"

The little girl looked at the pouch, her mouth and eyes wide open.

"Take this and give it to them."

"Really?"

Moncha thought for a second and sighed.

"Yes, really."

The girl took the pouch from her, "but, you must remember, you are not all wicked, little one. You are a little girl who makes mistakes, and even does wrong things, but you are not *only* what they say about you." Moncha smiled down at her and put her hand on her head.

"Who are you? Where did you come from?" the little girl asked.

"I'm not sure. My name is Moncha."

The little girl looked shocked. "That's my name."

Moncha started to cry.

"Is it? Is it really little one?"

She took the child in her arms and just held her. She wished she could rescue her. She wished she could get the King of Glory to come and take this little one to the Kingdom of Light. Would he ever find this little one? She did not know. Should she tell her about him? Moncha felt a steadiness in her heart she had not felt for days. She took the bucket from the girl and said, "Come on, lead me to your house, but make sure no one sees us. I will bear this heavy burden for you at least this one night."

Little Moncha took her hand and led her to her house. As they walked, Moncha told her the legend of the One and Only. When they were in sight of the house she stopped and knelt down by the little girl.

"If you ever see the One and Only, the King of Glory, you must go with him little one. He can rescue you from

104

this place. He…" she paused, "he loves you and wants you to be with him."

Little Moncha took a few steps back.

"How do you know that?"

"Because I have met him," Moncha said with tears in her eyes. "I have met him," she whispered to herself.

Little Moncha started to ask something else, but Moncha put her finger to her lips.

"No more now, you need to go inside or they will certainly be angry you've taken so long."

Little Moncha took a deep breath and said, "All right." She turned to go, holding the full bucket with both hands and struggling to walk. Moncha longed to keep her safe; to hold her forever.

But she did not have the power. She had done what she could do, she had told her about the one who could help.

As Moncha walked away, the reality of what she had done hit her. She sat down on a rock and wept. All her money was gone. She was alone and penniless. What could she do now? Why had she given all her money away? And yet, she did not regret it. It was the best thing she had ever done for anyone in her life. She realized she would not change it for anything.

What had happened to her? She was confused. She was different somehow.

Then, she thought about the mirror in her pocket. She took it out and struggled to see herself in the dim light of the moon. Her heart sank back into its familiar despair. No, no change. She was just as she always had been.

CHAPTER XX

She walked on and slept in a pile of hay for the night. In the morning, she went to the tavern and asked for a job. They told her she could scrub floors, wash dishes and fetch water in exchange for one meal a day and a place to sleep. She had no choice, and so she worked. In the evening, the place was busy. They told her if she'd help wait on tables, she could get an additional meal for the day. Moncha was exhausted, but her hunger was worse than her fatigue, so she agreed. She carried tray after tray of food and ale to the hungry and thirsty customers.

At one table sat a group of men who were evidently celebrating a day of successful trading. Moncha eyed one of the men's money pouches. It hung almost completely out of his pocket. She longed for that money. Money could buy her freedom from noisy villages. Then, just as she walked by, the pouch dropped to the floor. Without a thought, she swept it up in her hand and pretended to wipe up a mess on the floor. She had done this so many times in her life, it was a well-practiced maneuver. But when she turned to leave the table, a man was in her way. He grabbed her hand and said, "What'ya thinks you're doing missy?"

"What do you mean?"

"I saw you take his money. Give it back!"

He was shouting at her and drawing attention. Soon all the men at the table were standing up with menacing looks on their faces. The commotion drew the attention of the tavern owner.

"I say, what's going on over here?"

"Your girl here, she took his money. I saw her!" the man accused again.

Moncha had at one time talked her way out of more difficult situations than this, but as she searched her mind, she couldn't come up with anything. She stood speechless, and slipped her hand into her pocket and brought out the pouch of money. The tavern owner grabbed it from her hands. He looked at it, then at Moncha, and then he started to raise his hand to strike her, but another man held his hand back.

"I don't think you need to do that. Desmond has his money back, and we'd like to have another round ... on me."

The tavern owner put on a big smile.

"Sure thing, I'll have that out to you fine gents in no time!"

Then, he grabbed Moncha by the back of her dress, dragged her through the kitchen to the back door and threw her out.

"Try to steal from my customers, will ya? You're lucky you're getting out of here with your life!" And he slammed the door in her face.

Moncha took two steps back and turned around. She started running again and ran right out of the village. She was exhausted, hungry and thirsty. She kept running as long as she could, but soon her legs gave out from beneath her. She was falling. She rolled over to the side of the road, and her searching hands found a dry ditch beside her. She laid down in it, hoping she was out of sight, and instantly fell asleep. When she woke in the morning, she heard the clip-clop of a cart coming down the street. She poked her head up out of the ditch and saw it coming toward her from the direction of the village. She was too tired to walk, but she needed to get out of there. She waited until it passed, and then she climbed out of the ditch and jumped into the back, under the covers. As she lay there, she smelled the sweet aroma of apples and moved her hand until she felt a basket next to her. She reached her hand into the basket, pulled an apple out and ate it, core and all. She ate two more then fell asleep.

When she woke up again, the cart was still. She listened for voices, but they were in the distance. It must be night. She snuck out from under the covers and crept to the trees near the road. She was in a different village. This one was familiar. She had lived here for the past couple of years. This is where she had lived with Locke.

"Should I try to find him?" she wondered. "Would he take care of me?" She sat in the woods, listening to her own breathing and trying to figure out her next move. Just then, she saw Locke leaving the tavern across the street. She acted impulsively and ran over to him. "Locke!" she cried.

He stopped walking and looked up.

"Well, lookey here. Where've you been, you little dirt mongrel?" He surveyed Moncha's torn gown, "Sure haven't found you a rich man to keep company with, have ya?"

He laughed at her. She humbled herself and swallowed his comments as she always had.

"Locke, I am sorry. I just ... I just was gone."

"Ya left, you mean?!"

He shouted so all the people around them could hear.

"No matter! You weren't nothin' to me anyway."

He sneered and began walking away.

"Locke, I'm…" Moncha searched frantically for what to say, "I'm back. I'm back for you…"

"For me, is it? Well, wasn't your other man enough for ya? Didn't he treat you nice and give you fine clothes to wear?" He looked at her again, laughed and began walking off.

Moncha didn't know what to do, so she followed him.

"Maybe if things aren't so public he will take me back," she thought. He walked back to his crumbling dwelling. Moncha thought that he must know she was following him. She kept her distance and continued behind him. As he reached the door, he turned back.

"If ya get the water, you can stay the night…out here!" he said, pointing to the dirt in front of the door. Then, laughing to himself, he went inside and threw out the bucket and slammed the door.

Moncha took the bucket in her hand. She started to weep, but then drew back the tears. Had there ever been a time that he had loved her or cared about her? Then, a new thought came to her. She wondered if it had hurt him when she left. Underneath all that hate, was he vulnerable to rejection? She thought of how she had been treated her whole life and how it left her hardened to the world…could that be true of Locke, too? She sighed. Everything about life here was painful. Why had she wanted to come back so much? It was awful. Everything was darkness and loneliness. She longed for her talks with the Counselor, for her walks with the King of Glory. She missed having a song of praise in her heart. She was tired of being mad at the King.

As she neared the familiar spring, where she met Saoirse and the King of Glory, she wondered if she had been right. Had the King really lied to her, or could she change? Why didn't her mirror ever show any transformation?

"If only I hadn't left. Could I ever go back? But I have stolen from him. I took a crown. How could he forgive me?"

She looked at the bucket in her hand and sighed, "I would give anything just to be the one who brings him the water he drinks."[226]

CHAPTER XXI

When Moncha reached the spring, she knelt down and put her bucket under the flow of water to fill it up. She watched and waited as the fresh fountain bubbled over.

All at once she became aware of a light shining around her. Her heart jumped, and she looked up.

"Could it be?" she wondered, and then she saw him. The King of Glory on his horse, looking serious and intent.

"Oh, King of Glory!" she said and she knelt down before him. "I am so, so sorry," she said, crying.

She was afraid to look him in the eyes and terrified because she did not have the crown she had stolen.

"He must have come all this way to retrieve it," she thought, "and I do not have it. What will he do?"

He was getting off his horse.

"Kamea."

Moncha was startled to hear him use that name.

"Kamea, please get up and look at me."

His voice sounded both loving and strong.

She sat up and rose to her feet, but she was afraid to look at him.

"Kamea, Kamea, why have you run away?"

"Doesn't he know what I have done with his crown?" she wondered to herself.

"I ... I stole from you, King of Glory," she blurted out.

"What did you steal from me, little one?" he said.

"I stole a crown."

"How did you do that?"

Moncha was getting flustered. Where was this going?

"I just opened the cabinet and took it, and ran away."

"That is not what I meant, Kamea," the King of Glory said. "How could you steal what I had given you as a gift?"

Kamea did not know what to think about what he was saying. The King of Glory was nearing her with every breath, and he now put his hand under her chin and drew her eyes up to his face. He was not angry, but he was serious.

"How could you take what I had already generously given you?"

"But I did. I did it to run away."

"Why did you run away?"

"I had to."

"Why did you have to run away, Kamea? Why did you have to try to steal what I wanted to give to you? Why do you do these things?"

Kamea sensed a steady patience in his voice.

"Well, I have to. It is who I am. I can't help it. I loved you so, and I still messed up ... I still hurt you. I am wicked, through and through. I can't be reformed or changed. I am not like the other people in the Kingdom of Light. I will always be what I have been from the beginning ... wicked."

"No, Kamea, you have been wrong from the beginning. Your mirror, the one you have had since your youth, the one you have clung to and trusted – even after coming to my kingdom – that mirror has always been distorted. You have been my creation, the object of my love and mercy from the beginning. We had been separated by your evil deeds...but when you trusted me to save you,[227] when you

112

made me your Lord, that all was removed. You are washed clean[228]...you are a new creation."

Kamea felt frustration welling up inside of her.

"If that is true ... why do I do such wicked things[229] if I have been changed? Why do I still want to do bad things? Why do I still hurt people?" she retorted.

"You are a new creation. You are a daughter of mine. You are a citizen of my kingdom ... it is all true ... but you still have the ability to choose. You did wrong things because you chose to. It sometimes takes time for my newly adopted ones to realize they don't have to do evil anymore.[230] You actually did better than some. You stayed with me longer, and I enjoyed having you with me very much."

Kamea was confused by all this.

"Better than some? What..."

"You will have to accept that you will never deserve to be in my kingdom. You were never allowed in because of what you did. Entrance is through grace and faith alone!"[231]

"I betrayed you, I left you ... I hated you. I took your gift and I sold it." She sat down on an old log and hid her face in her hands, tears of shame blinding her eyes.

The King of Glory sat next to her.

"I know, Kamea. I have always known. Remember, all your days were laid out before me before one of them came to be.[232] I have known all these things and still, I have loved you. He paused and then posed this question, "Do you know which crown you took with you? Which one it was?"

"Yes," Kamea said, "the crown of compassion."

"Yes," he said taking a deep breath. "Do you know what compassion means?"

Kamea was struggling through her tears. "No," she realized. "No, I don't. Not really."

"Compassion means, 'with suffering.'[233] My father and I are gracious and compassionate, little one, slow to anger

113

and abounding in love.[234] I always knew that loving you would involve suffering, and I chose to love you anyway."

Kamea's mind was reeling, her thoughts were spinning. He always knew she would cause him to suffer, to sacrifice, to hurt, and yet he loved her anyway?

"And, dear Kamea, you have learned this love. You *have* changed. I have seen it."

"What do you mean?" she asked, looking away from him, overwhelmed and frustrated.

"You took the crown of compassion and sold it." He paused and took a breath. "And then, you took that money and gave it to one who needed it."

Kamea's heart began to pound, and the hairs on the back of her neck stood up. Tears were coming to her eyes.

"You suffered for that dear little child, and you were happy to do it."

Kamea started sobbing. She saw it; she saw what he meant.

"That was my love, Kamea, my compassionate love that came through you to that girl. You have been changed. All who are loved by my father and I are changed. You have begun to transform."

Kamea could not deny it. She could not explain why she would be so selfless toward that little girl. She thought of all the suffering: the work, the hunger, sleeping in the woods, and yet ... she was glad to have done it.

GLAD.

She would have done it again. This was not a love she had been shown as a child. This was not how she would have behaved even a few months ago. She would not have even noticed little Moncha back then. She had been changed. Something had happened to her. Then, she thought of the other things she had done.

"I tried to go back to stealing, to go back to Locke, but none of it worked – nothing helped. It was all ruined for me."

114

"Once you have tasted the life that is truly life, it ruins you for anything else," he said.

She could sense his smile. "You are not who you were, little one. The old is gone and the new has come!"[235]

"But, what should I do now? I do not fit in here ... I have nothing here, and yet, how could I go back to the Kingdom of Light after rejecting you and hating you so?" Kamea asked, crying again from her shame.

"If you claimed you were perfect and never did wrong, you would be a liar ... but as you confess your wrongdoing now, I will be faithful to forgive you and make you clean.[236] Would you like to be forgiven?"

Kamea thought of the first time she had met Saoirse and how she had talked of forgiveness, saying,

"Forgiveness means that even though what I did was wrong, and ought not to have been done, you will not hold it against me or make me pay for it in any way; that you will...that you will be generous and let it go."

"Kamea, I will cleanse you from all your crimes and wrongdoing. It will be removed from you so far it will be as far as the east is from the west."[237]

"I would like that so much," she said, crying.

Could it be real? Could it be possible to be truly purified like that? She wanted to believe it, but it seemed improbable.

"Kamea, I will always come for you ... my love always hopes, it never gives up ... it never fails."[238]

She drank in those words and continued to cry.

"I invite you now to come with me to the Kingdom of Light ... but I ask you, first, to break your old mirror and leave it behind."

Kamea looked at him, shocked that he would bring up the mirror.

"Kamea, you must walk in trust[239] or you will end up back in the Dominion of Darkness once more. You must

115

walk in faith or there will always be death and doubt in your heart. As you trust that you are who I say you are, as you believe me and get to know me, you will become more and more the person that I have made you to be."[240]

Darkness began to close in on Kamea again as she put her hand down to touch her mirror, "But ... why, when I look into my mirror…"

"You must trust me above all else. What reason do you have to believe that the mirror is being truthful to you? Why do you believe what it shows you above what I have told you?"

Kamea looked down; she was considering what he was saying. These were fresh thoughts to her mind.

"How do I know my mirror is truthful? I have always assumed it was, it has always said the same thing…but what if the mirror in the Kingdom of Light was the truthful one?"

"What will you believe? The reflections from the past, or the truth I speak to you now? I will complete this transformation I have begun in you.[241] I will give you the power to want what I desire[242] and the power to do what I want you to do,[243] to do what is good."

"I would like that, I think, but would I be free?"

"Wickedness is slavery Kamea ... those who do evil are slaves to evil. Those who follow the One and Only are the freest[244] people of the world. They can do the good they desire to do, because the evil sickness in them is defeated."

Kamea thought about what he said. She had run away, back to the Dominion of Darkness, to be free ... but had not found freedom; only fear, dread and darkness. She did not see freedom in the people here. They all served something: money, attention, distraction, comfort ... they were not free. Freedom was being able to help someone like little Moncha ... to do the good that you want to do.

"I am free from ever having to do wrong again?"

"Yes, little one. You see, I didn't just suffer to pay for your evil deeds; I conquered death so that you may be free of the power causing you to do wrong. Dear one, you do not ever have to do wrong again."

"I don't?"

"No. You have a choice. I can help you stand against every evil temptation.[245] You ARE free ... but you have yet to walk fully in that freedom."

She was on her knees now, crying and turning away in shame once again.

"I want that more than anything, but it is too good to be true," she whispered.

All at once, there was a brilliant light from behind her. As she turned, she saw the glorified King many times his normal size and so brilliant she could not behold him.

She could see now that his garments and appearance had changed. His head and hair were white like snow, and his eyes were like blazing fire. He had a sash about his chest and wore a long robe that reached to his feet and it read:

"King of Kings and Lord of Lords."

His face was like the sun, shining in all its brilliance.[246]

Kamea fell to her knees at the sight. As he spoke, his voice was like that of the rushing waters:

"I AM WHO I AM.[247] I AM NOT A MAN THAT I SHOULD LIE.[248] I NEVER CHANGE. I AM ALWAYS THE SAME, YESTERDAY, TODAY AND FOREVER.[249] MY LOVE IS UNFAILING.[250] I AM GRACIOUS AND COMPASSIONATE, SLOW TO ANGER AND ABOUNDING IN LOVE.[251] I HAVE RESCUED YOU."[252]

Though she was terrified, her heart burst with joy.

"You are the one I have waited for! You are the one I have longed for! You are the only Lord!"

She was already on her knees and as she pressed her forehead firmly to the ground, bright light was all around her and a holy presence filled the place.

"I am sorry, Lord, that I did not know you."

Tears of joy and awe were streaming down her face, "You are the One. You are the only One."

She paused.

"You are my Only One … and I love you."

While she was still bowing, she slid her old mirror slowly out of her pocket. It was time to be done with it.

She kept her head down as she raised the mirror up into the glory of her Lord. It shattered immediately, the pieces of glass cascading down all around her. She wept, feeling the freedom. She could not turn back now. It was finished. She was going to trust what the One and Only said about her – not the reflections of the past.[253]

She took his hand, and they walked back toward his horse. As Kamea walked by the stream, she noticed her reflection. She shone brightly,[254] just like the King of Glory! Her face was radiant; not a hint of shame.[255]

She smiled.

The old mirror, her companion since her youth, had lied to her by not showing her the whole truth. Perhaps she never really had seen herself truthfully before. She had been wicked; an enemy of the King of Glory, a rebel against the Almighty One, and so in that way the mirror had shown her the truth. Before she met the King of Glory, she had been covered with shame, dirtied by her wicked deeds, selfish and cold … but even then, the mirror had not shown her the glimmer of beauty – the mark of the Creator King that she had seen even in little Moncha. It had failed to show her the possibility, the potential that she could be transformed and become a citizen of the Kingdom of Light.

And then, after she had been rescued by the King of Glory, the mirror still reflected her old nature – which she, like all of the citizens of the Kingdom of Light, still carried with her. But it failed to reveal the new creation, which was now her true self. It revealed her old self, but did not reflect the newness, the transformation the King of Glory had brought to her life. Now, it was obvious to her: she was transformed. She was a new creation.[256]

118

And so, the mirror had to be destroyed so Kamea no longer would gaze into the old, deceptive and flawed reflection of herself, but instead fix her eyes[257] on what the King of Glory's true mirror revealed about her – the far greater and enduring image of who she was and who she was becoming: her truest self.

They mounted the horse together, and the King of Glory took her back out of the Dominion of Darkness, guided by his light, for it is never dark when you are with him. The road was again difficult, but they traveled easily and with great speed.

"Thank you for rescuing me … again," she said to him as they rode.

"I told you I would always come for you." He looked back at her. "My love never fails."

Kamea returned to the Kingdom of Light, to get to know and serve the One and Only. She grew in the knowledge of the Truth and was transformed to be more and more like the King with ever-increasing glory; [258] enjoying the delights of his presence and his unfailing love.

Epilogue

One day, there was a dirty, wicked, slothful man laying in the mud at the side of a road. He had given up all hope and wanted to die. There was no one left in the whole Dominion of Darkness that loved him. He questioned whether anyone ever had. All he had known in life was darkness, doubt and dread. Death was closing in around him.

Then he heard a horse coming.

"Perhaps they will show pity and ride over me and do me in!" he thought.

The horse's steps slowed, and then stopped just before his feet. "The constable!" he thought. "Looking to beat me and throw me in jail. Let him do his worst. It doesn't matter anymore."

"You there!"

It was a woman's voice. He slowly turned his face, his dirty hair hanging in matted locks, hampering his view. Then he saw her. She was radiant. Her hair shimmered and her smile shone. Her eyes sparkled, and there was a sweet contentment about her. She was beautiful. She got off her horse and came down into the dirt and the mud puddles where the man was laying. She knelt, her white, glittering gown getting soiled by the filth, and took his hand.

"You look thirsty ... here, drink this."

He stared at her, bewildered. She took a string off her shoulder that held a skin filled with revitalizing spring water and offered him some. She held his head and poured the cool, fresh water into his mouth. He drank, and it refreshed him enough that his eyes brightened and he sat up. He eyed the woman suspiciously.

She returned his gaze and spoke.

"Come, meet the one who will satisfy your every thirst. Let me introduce you to the One we have waited for. He told me everything I ever did,"[259] she said, her eyes full of hope, "and yet he showed me love and compassion I had never known. He is the mighty One who saves.[260] I was where you are, and he has rescued me and made all things new! He suffered to pay for all our wrongdoing, and offers us forgiveness ... the most wonderful and precious gift! He has the power to give you a new life. He has sent me to tell you so that you would come to him. He wants you to join him in his family, as I have. Come meet the King of Glory of the Kingdom of Light ... Come."

Her voice was soft, but it had an unmistakable authority.

Looking intently at him, tears twinkling in the corners of her eyes, Kamea gently said, "Come."

A Note from Jeri Howe

Why I wrote Kamea

Kamea is a tale that probably has some of my story in it. Okay, I know it does. But it also has some of what I've learned from other people's stories as well. It's all about trying to figure out who I am, and how becoming a Christian has changed me. I mean, if being a Christian is all about new life – what does that mean?

Kamea is designed to address questions such as:

- How can I be a new creation if I still do the same old, bad stuff?
- Where do I look to find out if I matter? If I am significant?
- What if I've run away from God? What if I'm mad at Him?
- What am I worth?
- What does forgiveness mean?

Like Kamea, I came to a time in my life when I felt that God led me to start challenging all the old beliefs I had about myself ... to start challenging my internal "mirror messages." I started to learn what the Word of God said about me, and compared that to what I had believed for years. Then, I had to make a choice. Would I exchange the old, familiar, internal "mirror messages" for what the Bible had to say? Would I allow the Word of God to "reflect" my identity and worth to me, or would I continue on the path I was on? As a result of the way I was living, my mind was full of confusion, but the Bible promised a mind of "life and peace" (Romans 8:6). I started trying to "think God's thoughts"[1] by meditating on the scriptures about me in the Bible. I decided to trust God's Word over the poisonous, familiar "mirror messages" I was so used to.

I began looking at the Word of God and putting my trust in what it said about me instead of what I had believed all my life. Instead of believing "I don't matter," I put my trust in the truth that I mattered so much to God that He gave his only son so that I would not die but have eternal life (John 3:16). I actually wrote down verses from the Bible on note cards and memorized them. I carried the cards with me everywhere and I tried to replace these old internal "mirror messages" in my mind with the truth from God's Word. I could not figure out another way to "think God's thoughts" than to memorize and ponder his Word, so that is what I endeavored to do. And God changed me.[2] It took some time, and Kamea's journey takes some time. But, I have been transformed ...God has set me free from so much of the depression and anxiety that used to plague my life. And I continue to be transformed by my merciful, powerful, loving God.

You can join the journey of transformation by continuing with Kamea through the companion Bible study, the KAMEA JOURNEY GUIDE.

In the *Reflections Studies*, found in the *Journey Guide*, you can join Kamea on this journey by identifying some

---

[1] This concept was introduced to me in the book *Battlefield of the Mind* by Joyce Meyer.

[2] I'd like to note that God used prayers — both mine and others' for me — good books, good friends, the support, teaching and ministry of my church and long walks in my healing as well.

of your own "mirror messages" and then comparing them to what the Word of God found in the Bible has to say about you. Where the messages contradict, you have an opportunity to "exchange mirrors" by putting your faith in what the Word of God says about you.

This can bring freedom from the haunting, negative "mirror messages" of the past. For many, adjusting what we believe about ourselves to line up with what God says about us in His Word will improve our emotional health, clear our minds for better decision-making and allow our hearts to accept the love that others, including God, offer us in relationships. It's a step toward healing, freedom and wholeness.

Come, journey alongside Kamea and be transformed by the renewing of your mind. (Romans 12:2)

Information on how to order the *Kamea Journey Guide* is available at kameathebook.com and jerihowe.com.

Register your copy of Kamea here to get updates and irregular messages from the author:

http://www.kameathebook.com/register.html

Endnotes:

From the Holy Bible (unless a name definition)

---

[1] See Genesis 1
[2] See Genesis 3
[3] See Isaiah 53:6
[4] See John 10:10
[5] See John 8:44
[6] See 1 John 5:19
[7] See Ephesians 6:12
[8] See Luke 1 & 2
[9] See Matthew 13:53-55
[10] See Hebrews 4:15
[11] See John 1:14-18, 3:16-18, 1 John 4:9
[12] See Isaiah 53:4-7
[13] See 2 Corinthians 5:21, 1 Peter 2:24, Isaiah52:14
[14] See Matthew 27:46
[15] See Matthew 27:50
[16] See Matthew 27:51
[17] See Matthew 28:1-8, Mark 16:1-8, Luke 24:1-10, John 20:1-8
[18] See 1 Corinthians 15:55-57
[19] See Matthew 28:16-20, Mark 16:9-20, Luke 24:13-35, Luke 24:36-49, John 20:10-18, 20:19-23, John 20:24-31, John 21:1-14, Acts 2:32
[20] See Colossians 1:13
[21] See Colossians 1:13
[22] See Matthew 4:16
[23] *Locke: pronounced "Lahk" meaning fortified place*
[24] See Ephesians 5:8
[25] *Saorise: pronounced "SEER sha," meaning freedom*
[26] See Psalm 24
[27] See Acts 2:38-39, Romans 9:25, John 6:44
[28] See John 17:2-3, 1 Timothy 2:3-4
[29] See John 17:24

[30] *Mara: pronounced "MAH rah" meaning bitter*
[31] See Psalm 103:12, 1 John 1:8-9
[32] See Mark 16:16, Acts 16:31, **Romans 10:9-10**,
Hebrews 10:39
[33] See Romans 6:6-11, 8:1-17
[34] See Colossians 1:13-14
[35] See Colossians 2:13-15
[36] See 1 Corinthians 1:18
[37] See John 4:1-26
[38] See Isaiah 53:2
[39] See John 4:18
[40] See John 4:29
[41] See Colossians 1:13
[42] See Galatians 5:1, Romans 6:22
[43] See Exodus 3:14
[44] See Isaiah 30:18
[45] See Romans 6:4
[46] See John 4:10, Romans 6:23, Romans 5:15-17
[47] Some people respond to Jesus' offer with a simple prayer. Here is one model of such a prayer:

**Dear God, I am sorry for the things that I have done wrong in my life.
(Take a moment to confess anything that is on your heart right now.)
I turn from these things to follow you in a new life.**

Lord Jesus, I believe that you died on the cross to pay the death penalty for me so that I could be forgiven and set free. I believe you rose again from the dead, for death could not hold you. I believe that you are now seated at the right hand of God, enthroned in power and glory. I believe you are who you say you are, the very Son of God, and the only way to God.

In the Bible, you promise that if I turn from my sins, and believe in you and what you have done for me, I'll receive new life and be saved from my sin and from death. Lord, I now turn, and I believe.

I thank you that, just as you promised, you now give me new life. Thank you that I am born anew by your Spirit and that my sins are forgiven. Thank you that I am now a member of your family. Thank you for giving me eternal life, and for the gift of your Spirit. I now receive that gift with joy.

In Jesus' name I pray, Amen.

(Acts 2:38, Acts 3:19-20, John 3:16-18, Acts 2:23-24, Colossians 3:1, John 14:6, John 11:25, Romans 10:8-11, John 3:3-8, John 4:14, John 7:38-39, Ephesians 1:4-5)

[48] See Isaiah 55:1-3
[49] See Ephesians 2:8-9
[50] See Psalm 139:11-12
[51] See John 4:17-19, 28-29
[52] See John 10:28-30
[53] *Kamea: pronounced "ka-MAY-ah"*
[54] See Psalm 105:43
[55] See Zephaniah 3:17
[56] See Psalm 24:7-10
[57] See Revelations 3:5, Ephesians 5:25-27
[58] See Psalm 34:5
[59] See Genesis 3:10
[60] See Isaiah 40:11
[61] See John 14:16, 26, 15:26, 16:7
[62] See John 16:13
[63] See Romans 1:18, 1:25, 2 Timothy 3:13

64 See 1 Timothy 6:17
65 See James 1:17
66 See Ephesians 1:5-6
67 *Adelaide: pronounced "ADD –eh-LADE" meaning noble, honorable*
68 See 2 Corinthians 5:17
69 See John 3:16-17
70 See Isaiah 53:6, Romans 3:23-24
71 See Philippians 3:19
72 See Romans 3:20
73 See Acts 4:12, John 14:6
74 See Romans 6:18, 22, Galatians 5:1
75 See Romans 6:23, Hebrews 9:22
76 See Galatians 4:7
77 See Ephesians 1:4-6
78 See Ephesians 5:1-2
79 See Isaiah 43:4
80 See 1 Peter 1:3-5
81 See Colossians 1:12
82 See Ephesians 2:8-9
83 See 2 Timothy 1:9
84 See 1 John 1:5
85 See 1 John 4:16
86 See Genesis 2:7, Romans 8:11
87 See Ephesians 2:19
88 See 1 Corinthians 13:12
89 See Colossians 3:12
90 See Ephesians 6:15
91 See Revelations 5:9
92 *Truman: pronunciation "TRU-man" meaning faithful man, trusted man*
93 See Colossians 3:23-24
94 See John 10:4
95 See Isaiah 40:11, Mark 9:36, 10:16
96 See Romans 14:8, Isaiah 43:1, 1 Corinthians 6:19-20

[97] See 1 Peter 2:9, Titus 2:13-14
[98] *Lamara: pronounced "la-MAR-ah" meaning bitter or sought-after child*
[99] See Romans 3:4, John 14:6
[100] See John 17:12, Jude 1:24-25
[101] See James 1:17
[102] See Isaiah 43:4,
[103] See Psalm 139:16
[104] See Psalm 56:8 (King James Version and New Living Translation include "put my tears in your bottle")
[105] See Matthew 10:30, Luke 12:7
[106] Zephaniah 3:17
[107] See Isaiah 30:21
[108] See Acts 1:15-17
[109] See Luke 19:10
[110] See Matthew 18:14, Luke 15:4
[111] *Rawiya: pronounced: "RAH wee yah" meaning storyteller, narrator*
[112] See John 10:10
[113] See John 14:26
[114] See Psalm 139:23, Romans 8:27
[115] See Psalm 139:4
[116] See John 2:25
[117] See Romans 5:8
[118] Psalm 139:16
[119] See Hebrews 4:13
[120] See Romans 3:23
[121] See 1 John 1:5
[122] See Psalm 147:11 (and many other Psalms!)
[123] See 1 Corinthians 15:55-57
[124] See Hebrews 13:8
[125] See John 15:15
[126] *Alwine: pronounced "al WEE neh" meaning noble friend*
[127] See Ephesians 2:13
[128] See Ephesians 3:12

[129] See 1 Timothy 6:17
[130] See 2 Corinthians 1:20, Romans 3:3-4
[131] See Isaiah 41:13
[132] See Ephesians 6:12
[133] See Colossians 1:21, Romans 5:10
[134] See Philippians 3:18-19
[135] See Ephesians 2:1-5
[136] See 1 Samuel 15:29
[137] See Romans 5:1,10-11
[138] See Ephesians 2:13
[139] See John 10:10
[140] See Ephesians 1:7-8, Colossians 1:14, 2:13-15
[141] See 1 John 3:9, 1 John 5:18
[142] See Psalm 68:20
[143] See John 19:30
[144] See Colossians 1:22
[145] See Isaiah 43:4
[146] See Isaiah 43:4
[147] See 2 Timothy 4:8
[148] See Colossians 1:12
[149] See Hebrews 4:16
[150] See Zephaniah 3:17
[151] See Psalm 84:11
[152] See Ephesians 1:7-8
[153] See 1 John 3:1, 2 Corinthians 6:18
[154] See Psalm 34:18
[155] See Psalm 139:5
[156] See Psalm 145:18
[157] See James 4:8
[158] See Jeremiah 31:3
[159] See John 6:44
[160] See Colossians 3:12
[161] See Psalm 91:4
[162] See Zephaniah 3:17
[163] See Ephesians 1:4

[164] See Romans 5:1
[165] See 2 Timothy 1:9
[166] See Psalm 46:10
[167] See Psalm 139: 13, 15-16
[168] See Psalm 139:4
[169] See 2 Timothy 2:19
[170] See 1 Corinthians 13:12
[171] See Psalm 27:10
[172] See Isaiah 41:10, Psalm 23:4, John 14:18
[173] See John 17:3, 1 John 5:20
[174] See Colossians 1:9-12
[175] See Ephesians 6:18, 1 Thessalonians 5:17
[176] See Ephesians 1:4
[177] See Psalm 139:13
[178] See Psalm 139:4
[179] See Psalm 27:10
[180] See Romans 12:19, Matthew 6:14-15, Matthew 18:21-22
[181] See James 1:20
[182] See 1 Peter 1:6, John 16:33
[183] See Psalm 42:2, 63:1, 143:6
[184] See Psalm 40:1-2
[185] See Zephaniah 3:17
[186] See Psalm 40:17
[187] See Matthew 15:3-5
[188] See Luke 15:3-7
[189] See Ephesians 5:2
[190] See Matthew 18:14
[191] See Ephesians 1:5
[192] See 1 Corinthians 7:23, Revelations 5:9
[193] See 2 Timothy 1:9
[194] See Psalm 40:1-3
[195] See Hebrews 12:7-11
[196] See Ephesians 5:2, 2 Timothy 3:16-17
[197] See Jude 1:24

[198] See Luke 15:7

[199] See Ephesians 2:1-3

[200] See John 8:34, Romans 6:16

[201] *Chapman: pronounced "CHAP-man" meaning trader, merchant*

[202] See Colossians 2:13, 1 Corinthians 15:22, Ephesians 2:4-5

[203] See 2 Corinthians 5:17

[204] See 1 Timothy 6:19, John 10:10

[205] See 2 Corinthians 4:6, Ephesians 5:8

[206] See Ephesians 4:28, 2 Thessalonians 3:6-10

[207] See Genesis 2:15

[208] See Ephesians 4:7-16

[209] See 2 Timothy 2:13

[210] See John 4:1-26

[211] See John 4:13-14

[212] See John 10:10

[213] See Matthew 28:18-20

[214] See Colossians 3:23-24, Romans 12:1

[215] See 2 Corinthians 5:17

[216] See Ephesians 5:27

[217] See 1 John 3:1-3

[218] See Psalm 34:5

[219] See 1 Peter 1:1, 2:11

[220] See Romans 5:5

[221] See 1 John 1:7, John 3:19-21

[222] See Ephesians 2:3

[223] See Romans 3:12

[224] See Ephesians 1:4-5, Psalm 139:13-16

[225] See John 3:16

[226] See Luke 15:16-20

[227] See Colossians 1:14, Ephesians 2:13

[228] See 1 Corinthians 6:11, Ephesians 5:26-27

[229] See Romans 7:14-24,

[230] See Romans 6:18, 22

231 See Ephesians 2:8-9

232 See Psalm 139:16

233 Compassion: from Latin: "com" meaning "with," and "pati" meaning "suffer, bear"

234 See Exodus 34:6

235 See 2 Corinthians 5:17

236 See 1 John 1:8-10

237 See Psalm 103:12

238 See 1Corinthians 13:7-8

239 See 2 Corinthians 5:7, Galatians 2:20

240 See Romans 12:2

241 See Philippians 1:6

242 See Philippians 2:13

243 See 1 John 3:9, 5:18, Romans 6:18, 22

244 See Galatians 5:1

245 See 1 Corinthians 10:13

246 See Revelation 1:12-18

247 See Exodus 3:14

248 See Numbers 23:19

249 See Hebrews 13:8

250 See Psalm 33:5

251 See Exodus 34:6

252 See Colossians 1:13

253 See Philippians 3:12-14

254 See Exodus 34:35

255 See Psalm 34:5

256 See 2 Corinthians 5:17

257 See 2 Corinthians 4:16-18

258 See 2 Corinthians 3:18

259 See John 4:28-29

260 See Zephaniah 3:17

Made in the USA
Coppell, TX
17 December 2019

13112995R00085